PRAISE FOR PETER V. BRETT

On *The Warded Man*,
Book One of The Demon Cycle

"I enjoyed *The Warded Man* immensely. There is much to admire in Peter Brett's writing, and his concept is brilliant. There's action and suspense all the way, plus he made me care about his characters and want to know what's going to happen next."
—Terry Brooks, author of the Shannara series

"*The Warded Man* works not only as a great adventure novel but also as a reflection on the nature of heroism."
—Charlaine Harris, author of the Sookie Stackhouse series

"An absolute masterpiece. . . . The novel [is] literally 'unputdownable,' and certainly deserves to be the next Big Thing in dark fantasy."
—*HorrorScope*

On *The Desert Spear*,
Book Two of The Demon Cycle

"Peter V. Brett is one of my favorite new authors."
—Patrick Rothfuss, *New York Times* bestselling author of *The Name of the Wind*

"The most significant and cinematic fantasy epic since *The Lord of the Rings*. Inspired, compelling, and totally addictive!"
—Paul W. S. Anderson, director of *Resident Evil: Afterlife*

**On *The Daylight War*,
Book Three of The Demon Cycle**

"Climaxing in a breathless confrontation between Arlen and Jardir and ending with a bang, this volume will leave series fans impatient for more."
—*Booklist*

"[Brett is] at the top of his game. I give this my highest recommendation."
—*Tor.com*

"[Brett] confirms his place among epic fantasy's pantheon of greats amid the likes of George R. R. Martin, Steven Erikson, and Robert Jordan."
—*Fantasy Book Critic*

The Great Bazaar & Brayan's Gold

PETER V. BRETT

OTHER BOOKS IN THE DEMON CYCLE

To Matt

Cover and interior design by Elizabeth Story.

Tachyon Publications
1459 18th Street #139
San Francisco, CA 94107
(415) 285-5615
tachyon@tachyonpublications.com

www.tachyonpublications.com
smart science fiction & fantasy

Series Editor: Jacob Weisman
Project Editor: Jill Roberts

ISBN 13: 978-1-61696-197-8

Printed in the United States of America by Worzalla

9 8 7 6 5 4 3 2

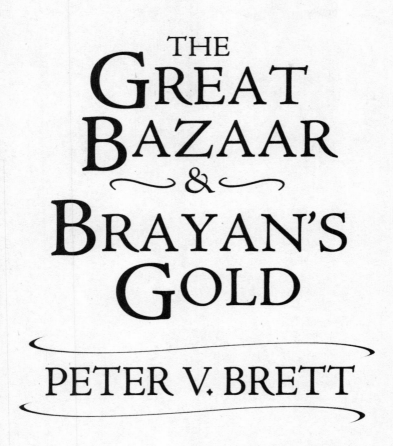

THE GREAT BAZAAR & BRAYAN'S GOLD

PETER V. BRETT

tachyon ✦ san francisco

TABLE OF CONTENTS

Introduction to
BRAYAN'S GOLD

It's all Matt's fault.

Seriously. This novella probably wouldn't exist had not my friend and longtime beta-reader, Matt Bergin, demanded it.

He had been reading an early draft of *The Great Bazaar*, and in it, I have Arlen reference one of his past misadventures where he encounters a snow demon without having the proper wards to protect himself.

"When did Arlen meet a snow demon?" Matt asked. "Did I miss that story?"

"There's no story," I said. "I just like reminding people that Arlen had a ton of adventures back when he was young and working for the Messengers Guild."

"Well, you've gotta write it, now," Matt said.

"Why?" I asked. I kind of liked the cryptic reference.

"Dude," Matt said. "You're passing up a chance to write about snow demons?"

It was a compelling argument, but I was swamped and couldn't get to it. I put the idea aside for over a year, but that whole time, I kept thinking about damned snow demons, and knew I would soon have poor Arlen's teeth chattering.

In the short break I allowed myself between finishing *The Desert Spear* and formally starting *The Daylight War*, I wrote this story, *Brayan's Gold*, the second stand-alone tale set in the world of the Demon Cycle.

I really enjoy this format, as it gives me a chance to tell short adventure stories that don't fit into the larger novels, offering newcomers an introduction to the series and some of its characters, longtime readers a broader look at the world, and impatient fans a coreling fix in the long wait between novel publications.

This volume is extra-special, because in addition to the story, it includes wards by the incredibly talented Lauren K. Cannon (www.navate.com). Lauren has been illustrating my work ever since I first sold *The Warded Man* back in 2007, and has done amazing work bringing my symbol magic and characters to life.

So if you are a newcomer or an old friend, welcome. I hope you enjoy *Brayan's Gold*.

And if you don't ... blame Matt.

BRAYAN'S GOLD

324 AR

"Hold still," Cob grunted as he adjusted the armor.

"Ent easy when a steel plate's cutting into your thigh," Arlen said.

It was a cool morning, dawn still an hour away, but Arlen was already sweating profusely in the new armor—solid plates of hammered steel linked at the joints by rivets and fine interlocking rings. Beneath, he wore a quilted jacket and pants to keep the plates from digging into his skin, but it was scant protection when Cob tightened the rings.

"All the more reason to make sure I get this right," Cob said. "The better the fit, the less likely that will happen when you're running from a coreling on the road. A Messenger needs to be quick."

"Don't see how I'll be anything near quick wrapped in bedquilt and carrying seventy pounds of steel on my back," Arlen said. "And this corespawned thing's hot as firespit."

"You'll be glad for the warmth on the windy trails to the Duke's Mines," Cob advised.

Arlen shook his head and lifted his heavy arm to look at the plates where he had painstakingly fluted wards into the steel with a tiny hammer and chisel. The symbols of protection were powerful enough to turn most any demon blow, but as much as he felt protected by the armor, he also felt imprisoned by it.

"Five hundred suns," he said wistfully. That was how much the armorer had charged—and taken months in the making. It was enough gold to make Arlen the second-richest man in Tibbet's Brook, the town where he had grown up.

"You don't go cheap on things that might mean your life," Cob said. He was a veteran Messenger, and spoke from experience. "When it comes to armor, you find the best smithy in town, order the strongest they've got, and bugger the cost."

He pointed a finger at Arlen. "And always . . ."

". . . ward it yourself," Arlen finished with his master, nodding patiently. "I know. You've told me a thousand times."

"I'll tell it to you ten thousand more, if that's how long it takes to etch it into your thick skull." Cob picked up the heavy helmet and dropped it over

Arlen's head. The inside was layered in quilt as well, and it fit him snugly. Cob rapped his knuckles hard against the metal, but Arlen heard it more than he felt it.

"Curk say which mine you're off to?" Cob asked. As an apprentice, Arlen was only allowed to travel on guild business accompanied by a licensed Messenger. The guild had assigned him to Curk, an aging and often drunk Messenger who tended to work only short runs.

"Euchor's coal," Arlen said. "Two nights' travel." Thus far, he had only made day-trips with Curk. This was to be the first run where they would have to lay out their portable warding circles to fend off the corelings as they slept by the road.

"Two nights is plenty, your first time," Cob said.

Arlen snorted. "I stayed out longer than that when I was twelve."

"And came out of that trip with over a yard of Ragen's thread holding you together, I recall," Cob noted. "Don't go getting swollen because you got lucky once. Any Messenger alive will tell you to stay out at night when you *have* to, not because you *want* to. The ones that want to always end up cored."

Arlen nodded, though even that felt a little dishonest, because they both knew he *did* want to. Even after all these years, there was something he knew he needed to prove. To himself, and to the night.

"I want to see the higher mines," he said, which

was true enough. "They say you can look out over the whole world from their height."

Cob nodded. "Won't lie to you Arlen. If there's a more beautiful sight than that, I've never seen it. Makes even the Damaji Palaces of Krasia pale."

"They say the higher mines are haunted by snow demons," Arlen said. "With scales so cold your spit will crack when it hits them."

Cob grunted. "The thin air is getting to the folks up there. I Messaged to those mines a dozen times at least, and never once saw a snow demon, or heard tale of one that bore scrutiny."

Arlen shrugged. "Doesn't mean they're not out there. I read in the Library that they keep to the peaks, where the snow stays year round."

"I've warned you about putting too much faith in the Library, Arlen," Cob said. "Most of those books were written before the Return, when folks thought demons were just ale stories and felt free to make up whatever nonsense they saw fit."

"Ale stories or no, we wouldn't have rediscovered wards and survived the Return without them," Arlen said. "So where's the harm in watching out for snow demons?"

"Best to be safe," Cob agreed. "Be sure to look out for talking nightwolves and fairy pipkins, as well."

Arlen scowled, but Cob's laugh was infectious, and he soon found himself joining in.

When the last armor strap was cinched, Arlen

turned to look in the polished metal mirror on the shop's wall. He was impressive looking in the new armor, there could be no doubt of that, but while Arlen had hoped to cut a dashing figure, he looked more like a hulking metal demon. The effect was only slightly lessened when Cob threw a thick cloak over his shoulders.

"Keep it pulled tight as you ride the mountain path," the old Warder advised. "It'll take the glare off the armor, and keep the wind from cutting through the joints."

Arlen nodded.

"And listen to Messenger Curk," Cob said. Arlen smiled patiently.

"Except when he tells you something that I taught you better," Cob amended. Arlen barked a laugh.

"It's a promise," he said.

They looked at each other for long moments, not knowing whether to clasp hands or hug. After a moment they both grunted and turned away, Arlen for the door and Cob for his workbench. Arlen looked back when he reached the door, and met Cob's eyes again.

"Come back in one piece," Cob ordered.

"Yes, Master," Arlen said, and stepped out into the pre-dawn light.

Arlen watched the great square in front of the Messengers' Guildhouse as men argued with merchants and stocked wagons. Mothers moved about with their chalked slates, witnessing and accounting the transactions. It was a place pulsing with life and activity, and Arlen loved it.

He glanced at the great clock over the Guildhouse doors, its hands telling the year, month, day, and hour, down to the minute. There was another great clock at the Guildhouse in every Free City, all of them set to the Tender's Almanac, which gave the times of sunrise and sunset for the coming week that were chalked beneath the clock face. Messengers were taught to live by those clocks. Punctuality, or better yet early arrival, was a point of pride.

But Curk was always late. Patience had never been one of Arlen's virtues, but now, with the open road beckoning, the wait seemed interminable. His heart thudded in his chest and his muscles knotted with excitement. It had been years since he last slept un-protected by warded walls, but he had not forgotten what it was like. Air had never tasted so good as it had on the open road, nor had he ever felt so alive. So free.

At last, there was a weary stomp of booted feet, and Arlen knew from the smell of ale that Curk had arrived before he even turned to the man.

Messenger Curk was clad in beaten armor of boiled leather, painted with reasonably fresh wards. Not as strong as Arlen's fluted steel, but a good deal lighter and more flexible. His bald pate was ringed by long blond hair streaked with gray, which fell in greasy gnarls around a weathered face. His beard was thick and roughly cropped, matted like his hair. He had a dented shield strapped to his back and a worn spear in his hand.

Curk stopped to regard Arlen's shining new armor and shield, and his eyes took a covetous gleam for an instant. He covered it with a derisive snort.

"Fancy suit for an apprentice." He poked his spear into Arlen's breastplate. "Most Messengers need to *earn* their armor, but not Master Cob's apprentice, it seems."

Arlen batted the speartip aside, but not before he heard it scratch the surface he had spent countless hours polishing. Memories came to him unbidden: the flame demon he struck from his mother's back as a boy, and the long cold night they spent in the mud of an animal pen as the demons danced about testing the wards for a weakness. Of the night he had accidentally cut the arm from a fifteen-foot-tall rock demon, and the enmity it bore him to this day.

He balled a fist, putting it under Curk's hooked nose. "What I done or not ent your business, Curk. Touch my armor again and the sun as my witness, you'll be spitting teeth."

Curk narrowed his eyes. He was bigger than Arlen, but Arlen was young and strong and sober. Perhaps that was why he stepped back after a moment and nodded an apology. Or perhaps it was because he was more afraid of losing the strong back of an apprentice

Messenger when it came time to load and unload the carts.

"Din't mean nothin' by it," Curk grumbled, "but you ent gonna be much of a Messenger if you're afraid to get your armor scratched. Now lift your feet. Guildmaster wants to see us before we go. Sooner we get that done, sooner we can be on the road."

Arlen forgot his irritation in an instant, following Curk into the Guildhouse. A clerk ushered them right into Guildmaster Malcum's office, a large chamber cluttered with tables, maps, and slates. A former Messenger himself, the guildmaster had lost an eye and part of his face to the corelings, but he continued to Message for years after the injury. His hair was graying now, but he was still a powerfully built man, and not one to cross lightly. A wave of his pen could bring dawn or dusk to a Messenger's career, or crush the fortune of a great house. The guildmaster was at his desk, signing what seemed an endless stack of forms.

"You'll have to excuse me if I keep signing while we talk," Malcum said. "If I stop even for an instant, the pile doubles in size. Have a seat. Drink?" He gestured to a crystal decanter on the edge of his desk. It was filled with an amber liquid, and there were glasses besides.

Curk's eyes lit up. "Don't mind if I do." He poured a glass and threw it back, grimacing as he filled another near to the rim before taking his seat.

"Your trip to Duke's Coal is postponed," Malcum said. "I have a more pressing assignment for you."

Curk looked down at the crystal glass in his hand, and his eyes narrowed. "Where to?"

"Count Brayan's Gold," Malcum said, his eyes still on the papers. Arlen's heart leapt. Brayan's Gold was the most remote mining town in the duchy. Ten nights' travel from the city proper, it was the sole mine on the third mountain to the west, and higher up than any other.

"That's Sandar's run," Curk protested.

Malcum blotted the ink on a form, turning it over onto a growing stack. His pen darted to dip in the inkwell. "It was, but Sandar fell off his ripping horse yesterday. Leg's broke."

"Corespawn it," Curk muttered. He drank half his glass in one gulp and shook his head. "Send someone else. I'm too old to spend weeks on end freezing my arse off and gasping for breath in the thin air."

"No one else is available on short notice," Malcum said, continuing to sign and blot.

Curk shrugged. "Then Count Brayan will have to wait."

"The count is offering one thousand gold suns for the job," Malcum said.

Both Curk and Arlen gaped. A thousand suns was a fortune for any message run.

"What's the claw?" Curk asked suspiciously. "What do they need so badly it can't wait?"

Malcum's hands finally stopped moving, and he looked up. "Thundersticks. A cartload."

Curk shook his head. "Ohhh, no!" He downed the rest of his glass and thumped it on the guildmaster's desk.

Thundersticks, Arlen thought, digesting the word. He had read of them in the Duke's Library, though the books containing their exact composition had been forbidden. Unlike most other flamework, thundersticks could be set off by impact as well as spark, and in the mountains, an accidental blast could cause an avalanche even if the explosion itself didn't kill.

"You want a rush job, carrying thundersticks?" Curk asked incredulously. "What's the corespawned hurry?"

"Spring caravan came back with a message from Baron Talor reporting a new vein, one they need to blast into," Malcum said. "Brayan's had his Herb Gatherers working day and night making thundersticks ever since. Every day that vein goes uncracked, Brayan's clerks tally up the gold he's losing, and he gets the shakes."

"So he sends a lone man up trails full of bandits who will do most anything to get their hands on a cartload of thundersticks." Curk shook his head. "Blown to bits or robbed and left for the corelings. Hardly know which is worse."

"Nonsense," Malcum said. "Sandar made thunderstick runs all the time. No one will know what you're carrying save us three and Brayan himself. Without guards, no one seeing you pass will think you're carrying anything worth stealing."

Curk's grimace did not lessen. "Twelve hundred suns," Malcum said. "You ever seen that much gold in one place, Curk? I'm tempted to squeeze into my old armor and do it myself."

"I'll be happy to sit at your desk and sign papers, you want one last run," Curk said.

Malcum smiled, but it was the look of a man losing patience. "Fifteen, and not a copper light more. I know you need the money, Curk. Half the taverns in the city won't serve you unless you've got coin in hand, and the other half will take your coin and say you owe a hundred more before they'll tap a keg. You'd be a fool to refuse this job."

"A fool, ay, but I'll be alive," Curk said. "There's always good money in carrying thundersticks because sometimes carriers end up in pieces. I'm too old for demonshit like that."

"Too old is right," Malcum said, and Curk started in surprise. "How many message runs you got left in you, Curk? I've seen the way you rub your joints in bad weather. Think about it. Fifteen hundred suns in your accounts before you even leave the city. Keep away from the harlots and dice that empty Sandar's purse, and you could retire on that. Drink yourself into oblivion."

Curk growled, and Arlen thought the guildmaster might have pushed him too far, but Malcum had the look of a predator sensing the kill. He took a key from his pocket and unlocked a drawer in his desk, pulling out a leather purse that gave a heavy clink.

"Fifteen hundred in the bank," he said, "plus fifty in gold to settle your accounts with whichever creditor is lingering by your horse today, looking to catch you before you leave."

Curk groaned, but he took the purse.

They hitched their horses to Brayan's cart, but in Messenger style, kept them saddled and packed in addition to the yoke. They might require speed if a wheel cracked close to dusk.

The cart looked like any other, but a hidden steel suspension absorbed the bumps and depressions of the road with nary a jostle to the passengers and cargo, keeping the volatile thundersticks steady. Arlen hung his head over the edge to look at the mechanics as they rode.

"Quit that," Curk snapped. "Might as well wave a sign we're carrying thundersticks."

"Sorry," Arlen said, straightening. "Just curious."

Curk grunted. "Royals all ride around town in fancy carts suspended like this. Wouldn't do for some well-bred lady to ruffle her silk petticoats over a bump in the road, now would it?"

Arlen nodded and sat back, breathing deeply of the mountain air as he looked over the Milnese plain spread out far below. Even in his heavy armor, he felt lighter as the city walls receded into the distance behind them. Curk, however, grew increasingly agitated, casting suspicious eyes over everyone they passed and stroking the haft of his spear, lying in easy reach.

"There really bandits in these hills?" Arlen asked.

Curk shrugged. "Sometimes mine townies short on one thing or another get desperate, and *everyone* is short on thundersticks. Just one of the corespawned things can save a week's labor, and costs more than townies see in a year. Word gets out what we're carryin', every miner in the mountains will be tempted to tie a cloth across his nose."

"Good thing no one knows," Arlen said, dropping a hand to his own spear. But despite their sudden doubt, the first day passed without event. Arlen began to relax as they moved past the main roads miners used and headed into less-traveled territory. When the sun began to droop low in the sky, they reached a common campsite, a ring of boulders painted with great wards encircling an area big enough to accommodate a caravan. They pulled up and unhitched the cart, hobbling the horses and checking the wards, clearing dirt and debris from the stones, and touching up the paint where necessary.

After their wards were secure, Arlen went to one of the fire pits and laid kindling. He pulled a match from the drybox in his belt pouch and flicked the white tip with his thumbnail, setting it alight with a pop.

Matches were expensive, but common enough in Miln and standard supply for Messengers. In Tibbet's Brook where Arlen was raised, though, they had been rare and coveted, saved only for emergencies. Only Hog who owned the General Store—and half the Brook—could afford to light his pipe with matches. Arlen still got a little thrill every time he struck one.

He soon had a comfortable fire blazing, and panfried some vegetables and sausage while Curk sat with his head propped against his saddle, pulling from a clay jug that smelled more like an Herb Gatherer's disinfectant than anything fit for human consumption. By the time they had eaten, it was full dark and the rising had begun.

Mist seeped from invisible pores in the ground, reeking and foul, slowly coalescing into harsh demonic form. There were no flame demons in the cold mountain heights, but wind demons materialized in plenty, as did a few squat rock demons—no bigger than a large man, but weighing thrice as much, all of it corded muscle under thick slate armor. Their wide snouts held hundreds of teeth, bunched close like nails in a box. Wood demons stalked the night as well, taller than the rock demons at ten feet, but thinner, with barklike armor and branchlike arms.

The demons quickly caught sight of their campfire and shrieked in delight, launching themselves at the men and horses. Silver magic spiderwebbed through the air as the corelings reached the wards, throwing the force of the demons' attack back at them and knocking more than a few to the ground.

But the demons didn't stop there. They began to

circle, striking at the forbidding again and again as they searched for a gap in the field of protection.

Arlen stood close to the wards without shield or spear, trusting in the strength of the magic. He held a stick of graphite and his journal, taking notes and making sketches as he studied the corelings in the flashes of wardlight.

Eventually, the corelings tired of their attempts and went off in search of easier prey. The wind demons spread their great leathery wings and took to the sky, and the wood demons vanished into the trees. The rock demons lumbered off like living avalanches. The night grew quiet, and without the light of the flaring wards, darkness closed in around their campfire.

"Finally," Curk grunted, "we can get some sleep." He was already wrapped in his blankets, but now he corked his jug and closed his eyes.

"Wouldn't count on that," Arlen said, standing at the edge of the firelight and looking back the way they had come. His ears strained, picking up a distant cry he knew too well.

Curk cracked an eye. "What's that supposed to mean?"

"There's a rock demon coming this way," Arlen said. "A big one. I can hear it."

Curk tilted his head, listening as the demon keened again. He snorted. "That demon's miles from here, boy." He dropped his head back down, snuggling into his blankets.

"Don't matter," Arlen said. "It's got my scent."

Curk snorted, eyes still closed. "*Your* scent? What, you owe it money?"

Arlen chuckled. "Something like that."

Soon, the ground began to tremble, and then outright shake as the gigantic one-armed rock demon bounded into view.

Curk opened his eyes. "That is one big ripping rock." Indeed, One Arm was as tall as three of the rock demons they had seen earlier. Even the stump of its right arm, severed at the elbow, was longer than a man was tall. One Arm had followed Arlen ever since he had crippled it, and Arlen knew it would continue to do so until one of them was dead.

But it won't be me, he promised the demon silently as their eyes met. *If I do nothing else before I die, I will find a way to kill you.*

He raised his hands and clapped at it, his customary greeting. The coreling's roar split the night, and darkness vanished as the powerful demon struck hard at the wardnet with its talons. Magic flared bright and strong, throwing the demon back, but it only spun, launching its heavy, armored tail into the wards. Again the magic rebounded the blow. Arlen knew the shock of magic was causing the demon agonizing pain, but One Arm did not hesitate as it lowered its spearlike horns and charged the wards, causing a blinding flash of magic.

The demon shrieked in frustration and came again, circling and attacking with talon, horn, and tail in its search for a weakness, even smashing the stump of its crippled arm against the wardnet.

"It'll tire out and quit the racket soon enough," Curk grunted and rolled over, throwing the blanket over his head.

But One Arm continued to circle, hammering at the wards over and over until the wardlight seemed perpetual, the flashes of darkness like eye blinks. Arlen studied the demon in the illumination, looking for a weakness, but there was nothing.

Finally Curk sat up. "What in the Core is the matter with that crazy. . . ?" His eyes widened as he caught a clear look at One Arm. "That's the demon from the breach last year. The one-armed rock that stalks Jongleur Keerin for crippling it."

"Ent after Keerin," Arlen said. "It's after me."

"Why would it . . ." Curk began, but then his eyes widened in recognition.

"You're him," Curk said. "The boy from Keerin's song. The one he saved that night."

Arlen snorted. "Keerin couldn't save his own breeches from a soiling if he was out in the naked night."

Curk chuckled. "You expect me to believe you're the one that cut that monster's arm off? Demonshit."

Arlen knew he shouldn't care what Curk thought, but even after all these years, it grated on him that Keerin, a proven coward, had taken credit for his deed. He turned back to the demon and spat, his wad of phlegm striking the coreling's thigh. One Arm's rage quadrupled. It shrieked in impotent fury, hammering even harder at the wards.

All the color drained from Curk's face. "You crazy boy, provoking a rock demon?"

"Demon was already provoked," Arlen pointed out. "I'm just showing it's personal."

Curk cursed, throwing aside his blankets and reaching for his jug. "Last run I do with you, boy. Never get to sleep now."

Arlen ignored him, continuing to stare at One Arm. Hatred and revulsion swirled around him like a cloud of stink as he tried to imagine a way to kill the demon. He had never seen nor heard of anything that could pierce a rock demon's armor. It was only an accident of magic that severed the demon's arm, and not something Arlen would bet his life on the odds of repeating.

He looked back at the cart. "Would a thunderstick kill it, you think? They're meant to break rocks."

"Them sticks ent toys, you crazy little bugger," Curk snapped. "They can do ya worsen any rock demon. And even if you've got a night wish and want to try anyway, they ent ours. If they count sticks and it don't meet the tally that left Miln, even by one, it's worse for our reputation than if we lost the lot."

"Just wondering," Arlen said, though he cast a longing look at the cart.

It was quiet the next day, as they rode across the

southern base of Mount Royal—the western sister of Mount Miln—whose eastern facing was filled with small mining towns. But the number of signposts dwindled as they made their way to the western face, and the road became little more than wagon ruts leading a path through the wilderness, with a few rare forks.

Late in the day, they reached the point where Royal joined with the next mountain in the range, and there stood a great clearing surrounding a gigantic wardpost made of crete, standing twenty feet high. The wards were so large a whole caravan could succor underneath them.

"Amazing," Arlen said. "Must've cost a fortune to have that cast and hauled out here."

"A fortune to us is just copper lights to Count Brayan," Curk said.

Arlen hopped down from the cart and went over to inspect the great post, noting the hard way the dirt in the clearing was packed, indentations telling the tale of hundreds of fire pits and stakes put down by Messengers, caravan crews, and settlers over the years. The site was freshly used even now, smelling faintly of woodsmoke from a previous night's fire.

As he studied the wardpost, Arlen noticed a brass plaque riveted into the base of the post. It read: BRAYAN'S MOUNT.

"Count Brayan owns the whole mountain?" Arlen asked.

Curk nodded. "When Brayan asked permission to mine all the way out here, the Duke laughed and gave him the whole damn mountain for a Jongleur's song. Euchor didn't know that Countess Mother Cera, Brayan's wife, had found tale of a gold mine on the peak in an old history."

"Reckon he's not laughing now," Arlen said.

Curk snorted. "Now Brayan owns half the crown's debt, and Mother Cera's arse is the only one in the city Euchor's afraid to pinch." They both laughed as Arlen began to climb the post, clearing windblown leaves and even a fresh bird's nest from the wards.

It was a cold spring night, but the post radiated heat, drawn from the demons that attempted to breach its radius. The forbidding waned the further one got from the post, but it easily extended fifty feet in every direction. Even One Arm could not approach.

The next morning, they began to ascend the winding road that would twist around the entire mountain three times, getting ever narrower, rockier, and colder, before it brought them to Brayan's mine. It was around midday when they approached a large rock outcropping, and a shrill whistle cut the air. Arlen looked up just as something struck the bench between him and Curk, blasting through the wood like a rock demon's talon.

"That was just a sign to let you know we mean business," a man said, stepping out from around the rock face. He wore thick coveralls and a miner's helm with candle cup. A kerchief was tied across his nose to cover the rest of his face. "Fella atop them boulders can thread a needle with his crank bow."

Arlen and Curk glanced up and saw there was indeed a man kneeling atop the rocks, his face similarly covered as he pointed a heavy crank bow at them. A spent bow lay at his side.

"Corespawn it," Curk spat. "Knew this would happen." He lifted his hands high.

"He only has one shot," Arlen murmured.

"One's all he needs," Curk muttered back. "Crank bow this close'll go through even your fancy armor like it was made of snow."

They turned their eyes back to the man on the road. He carried no weapons, though he was followed by two men with hunter's bows nocked and drawn, and they by half a dozen thick-armed men with miner's picks. All wore the candled helms with kerchiefs across their faces.

"Ent lookin' to shoot anyone," the bandit leader said. "We ent corelings, just men with families to feed. Everyone knows you Messengers get paid in advance and keep your own bags on your horses. You unhitch that cart and go on about your business. We ent looking to take what's yours."

"I dunno," said one of the men with picks, as he strode up to where Arlen sat. "Might need to take that shiny warded armor, too." He tapped Arlen's breastplate with his weapon, putting a second scratch in the steel, next to the one Curk had made.

"The Core you will," Arlen said, grabbing the pick haft just under the head. He yanked it back and put his steel-shod boot in the face of the man as he was pulled forward. Teeth and blood arced through the air as the man hit the ground hard.

Arlen tossed the pick down the mountain and had his shield and spear out in an instant. "Only thing anyone comes near this cart will be taking is my spear in their eye."

"You crazy, boy?" Curk demanded, his hands still lifted. "Gonna get killed over a cart?"

"We promised to see this cart to Brayan's Gold," Arlen said loudly, never taking his eyes off the bandits, "and that's what we're going to do."

"This ent a game, boy," bandit leader said. "A crankbow bolt will punch right through that shield."

"Your bowman had best hope so," Arlen said, loud enough for the bowman to hear, "or we'll see if he can dodge a spear without falling off those rocks and breaking his neck."

The leader stepped up and grabbed the arm of the bandit Arlen had kicked, hauling him to his feet and shoving him back toward the others in one smooth motion.

"That one's an idiot," he told Arlen, "and he don't speak for us. I do. You keep your armor. We don't even need your cart. Just a few crates off the back, and we'll let you ride on safe and sound."

Arlen stepped into the back of the cart, putting his boot on a crate of thundersticks with a thump. "These crates? You want I should just kick 'em off the cart?" Curk gave a shout and backpedaled, falling from his seat. Everyone jumped.

The leader held up his hand, patting the air. "No one's sayin' that. You know just what it is you're carryin', boy?"

"Oh, I know," Arlen said. He kept his shield up as he squatted, setting down his spear and pulling out a thunderstick. It was two inches in diameter and ten long, wrapped in a dull gray paper that belied the power within. A thin fuse of slow burning twine hung from one end.

"I've a match, to go with it," Arlen said, holding the thunderstick up for all to see.

The bandits on the ground all took several steps back. "You be careful now, boy," the leader said. "Them things don't always need a spark to go off. Ent wise, swingin' it around."

"Best keep your distance, then," Arlen said. For a moment, silence fell as he and the bandit leader locked stares. Then came a sudden snapping sound, and everyone jumped.

Arlen looked over to see that Curk had cut his horse from the cart harness and was swinging into the saddle. He readied his spear and shield and turned to face the bandits. Arlen saw doubt in the bandit leader's eyes, and smiled.

But Curk kept his speartip down, and Arlen felt his momentary advantage vanish.

"Don't want no part of some thunderstick showdown!" Curk shouted. "I got years of drinking ahead of me, and fifteen hundred suns to pay for it!"

The bandit leader gave a start, but then he nodded. "Smart man." He signaled the others to move back, giving Curk an open path back down the road. "You stay smart, and keep on riding when you see the wardpost."

Curk looked at Arlen. "Can't handle a scratch on your armor, but you'll blow yourself to bits over a cart? You ent right in the head, boy." He kicked his horse hard, and in moments he had vanished back down the trail. Even the sound of his galloping hoofbeats quickly faded.

"Ent too late to do the same," the bandit leader said, turning back to Arlen. "You ever seen what a thunderstick can do to a man? What you've got in your hand'll blow you apart so there's nothing to burn at the funeral. Tear that pretty warded armor of yours like paper."

He gestured down the trail where Curk had ridden. "Get on your horse and go. You can even take that stick in your hand for insurance."

But Arlen made no move to get off the cart. "Who told you we were coming? Was it Sandar? If I find his leg ent really broken, I'll break it for him."

"Don't matter who told us," the bandit said. "No

one's going to think you didn't do your duty. You done Messengers proud, but you ent gonna win this. What do you care, if Count Brayan sees a dip in his ledgers? He can afford it."

"Don't care about Count Brayan," Arlen admitted. "But I care about my promises, and I promised to get this cart and everything on it to his mines."

The men spread out, three picks and a bowman at either end of the road. "That ent gonna happen," the bandit leader said. "You try to move that cart, we shoot your horse."

Arlen glanced at the bowmen. "Shoot my horse and it'll be the last thing you ever do," he promised.

The bandit sighed. "So where does that get us, 'cept half hour closer to dark?"

"How close are you willing to get?" Arlen asked. He rapped his gauntlet against his scratched breastplate. "I'll stand here in my 'pretty warded armor' right until the rising."

He looked out over the bandits, all of them on foot and none carrying so much as a pack. "You, I expect, need to get on back to succor at Brayan's Wardpost before dark. That's why you told Curk to keep on riding, and it's at least five hours' walk back the way we came. Wait too long, and you won't make it in time. Is it worth it to get cored over a few boxes of thundersticks when you have families to feed?"

"All right, we tried to do it easy," the bandit leader

said. "Fed, shoot him." Arlen ducked under his shield, but there was no immediate impact.

"You said no names, Sandar!" the crank bowman cried.

"Ent gonna matter, you idiot, once you put a bolt through his head," Sandar snapped.

Arlen started. Of course. He had never met Sandar, but it made perfect sense. He shifted his shield so he could see the bandit. "You faked the break so you could ride out a day early and ambush your own shipment."

Sandar shrugged. "Ent like you're gonna live to tell anyone."

But still there was no shot from above. Arlen dared to peek over his shield. Fed's hands shook, his aim veering wildly, and finally he put up the weapon.

"Corespawn it, Fed!" Sandar shouted. "Shoot!"

"Suck a demon's teat!" Fed shouted back. "I didn't come out here to shoot some boy. My son's older'n him."

"Boy had his chance to walk away," Sandar said. Some of the others grunted in agreement, including the man Arlen had kicked.

"Don't care," Fed called. "'No one gets hurt,' you said. 'Just a dip in some Royal's ledger.'" He pulled the bolt from his bow and slung the weapon over his shoulder, picking up the spare as well. "I'm done." He moved to pick his way down the outcropping.

One of the other bowmen eased his draw as well.

"Fed's right. I'm sick of eatin' gruel as anyone, but I ent lookin' to kill over it."

Arlen looked for the last bowman's reaction, but the man only sighted and fired.

He got his shield up in time, but it was a heavy bow, and the shield was only a thin sheet of hammered steel riveted onto wood, meant more to defend against corelings and nightwolves than arrows. The arrowhead made it through before the shaft caught fast, puncturing the side of Arlen's cheek. He stumbled back and almost lost his balance, squeezing the thunderstick so hard he was afraid it would go off in his hand. Everyone tensed.

But Arlen caught himself and straightened, turning to reveal the match clutched in his shield hand. He struck it with his thumb, and it lit with a pop.

"I'm going to light the fuse before the match burns my finger," he said, waving the thunderstick, "and then I'm going to throw it at anyone still in my sight."

A couple of men turned and ran outright. Sandar's eyes narrowed, but at last he lifted his kerchief to spit, and whistled for the rest to follow him as he headed down the road.

The match did end up burning Arlen's hand, but he never needed to light the fuse. A few minutes later, he was back on his way up the mountain. Dawn Runner was not pleased about pulling the entire load, but it could not be helped. He didn't think the bandits would be able to follow him on foot, but he kept the thunderstick and his drybox close to hand, just in case. It was nearing dark when he made it to the next wardpost.

Sandar was waiting.

The Messenger had shed his miner's disguise, clad now in battered steel mail and carrying a heavy spear and shield. He sat atop a powerful destrier, much larger than a sleek courser like Dawn Runner. With a horse like that, and no cart to slow him or limit his path, it wasn't surprising that he had gotten ahead of Arlen.

"Had to be a goody, dincha?" Sandar asked. "Couldn't leave it alone. Guild is insured. You're insured. You could've ridden off with Curk. The only loser would have been Count Brayan, and that bastard's got gold comin' out his arse."

Arlen just looked at him.

"But now," Sandar raised his spear. "Now I *have* to kill you. Can't trust you to keep your mouth shut otherwise."

"Any reason I should?" Arlen asked. "I don't take kindly to having bows aimed at me." He picked up the thunderstick sitting next to him in the driver's seat.

Sandar moved his horse closer. "Do it," he dared. "Blast this close'll set off every crate. Kill us both, and the horses besides. Either way, them sticks ent getting to Brayan's Gold."

Arlen looked him hard in the eyes, knowing he was right. Whatever Curk might think, he wasn't crazy, and didn't want to die today.

"Then get off your horse," Arlen said. "Fight me fair, and our spears can decide which of us walks away."

"Ent no one can say you ent got stones, boy," Sandar laughed. "If you want me to hand you a proper beating before I kill you, I'll oblige." He rode into the clearing by the wardpost, dismounting and staking down his horse. Arlen followed and set the thunderstick down, taking up his spear and shield before hopping down from the cart.

He set his feet apart in a comfortable stance, his shield and spear ready. He had practiced spearfighting with Cob and Ragen for countless hours, but this was real. This time, it would end in blood.

Like most Messengers, Sandar was built more like a bear than a man. His arms and shoulders were thick, with a barrel chest and a heavy gut. He held his weapons like they were a part of him, and his eyes had the dead, predatory stare of One Arm. Arlen knew he would not hesitate on the killing stroke.

They began to circle in opposite directions, eyes searching for an opening. Sandar made an exploratory thrust of his spear, but Arlen batted it aside easily and returned quickly to guard, refusing to be baited. He returned a measured thrust of his own. As expected, Sandar's shield snapped up to intercept.

Again Sandar attacked, this time more forcefully, but the moves were all simple spear forms. Arlen knew all the counters and picked them by rote, waiting for the real attack, the one that would come as

a surprise when he thought he was countering something else.

But that attack never came. Sandar was powerfully
built and had murder in his eyes, but fought like a
novice. After several minutes of dancing around the
wardpost, Arlen tired of the game and stepped into the
next predictable attack. He ducked, hooking Sandar's
shield with his own and raising both to cover himself
as he stomped on the side of the Messenger's knee.

There was a sharp snap that echoed in the crisp air,
like the branch of a winter-stripped tree breaking off
in the wind. Sandar screamed and collapsed to the
ground.

"Son of the Core! You broke my ripping leg!" he
howled.

"Promised I would," Arlen said.

"I'll kill you!" Sandar shrieked, writhing on the
ground in agony.

Arlen took a step back and raised his visor. "I don't
think so. Fight's over, Sandar. Sooner you realize that,
the sooner I can come set that leg for you."

Sandar glared at him, but after a moment, he threw
his spear and shield out of reach. Arlen put down his
own weapons and took Sandar's spear. He braced it
against the ground and snapped it with a sharp kick
of his steel-shod heel. He laid the two halves on the
ground by Sandar and knelt to examine the leg.

As he did, Sandar threw a fistful of loose dirt right
in his eyes.

Arlen gave a yell and stumbled back, but Sandar was on him in an instant, knocking him to the ground. Flat on his back in heavy steel armor with another man atop him, Arlen had no way to rise.

"Ripping kill you!" he screamed, hammering Arlen about the head with heavy gauntleted fists. Rather than crippling him, the pain in his leg seemed to give him a mad strength like a cornered nightwolf.

Arlen's head felt like the clapper from a bell, and it was impossible to think clearly. Half-blind from the grit, he felt more than saw the long knife that suddenly appeared in one of Sandar's fists. The first thrust skittered across his breastplate, and the next bit into the interlocking rings at his shoulder joint.

Arlen threw his head back and howled. The armor turned the edge, but the pain was incredible, and he knew his shoulder would ache for days.

That was, assuming he lived through the next few minutes.

Sandar gave up trying to pierce the armor and stabbed the knife at Arlen's throat. Arlen caught his wrist, and they struggled silently for the next few moments. Arlen strained every muscle he had, but Sandar had weight and leverage in addition to his mad strength. The blade drew ever closer to the thin but vulnerable seam between Arlen's neckplate and helmet.

"Almost there," Sandar whispered.

"Not quite," Arlen grunted, punching a mailed fist

into Sandar's broken knee. The Messenger screamed and recoiled in agony, and Arlen punched him full in the jaw, rolling as the man fell and reversing the pin. He pinned the knife arm with his knee, and landed several more heavy blows before the weapon fell from Sandar's limp hand.

Well after dark, Arlen sat by the edge of the wardnet, watching One Arm and holding the thunderstick thoughtfully. In his other hand, he held the white-tipped match. His fingers itched to light it, and his other arm tensed, ready to throw. He pictured One Arm catching the stick in its jaws, and the explosion blowing the demon's head apart. Pictured its headless body lying on the ground, oozing ichor.

But he kept hearing Curk's voice in his head. *Them sticks ent ours, boy.* Curk might have been a coward in the end, but he was right about that. Arlen was no thief. He glanced at Sandar, surprised to find the man awake and staring at him.

"Know what you're thinking," Sandar said, "but there's a lot of loose rock up mountain. Thunderstick's more likely to cause a landslide than kill that demon."

"You don't know what I'm thinking," Arlen said.

Sandar grunted. "Honest word," he agreed. "Been trying to figure out why you splinted my leg and put a cold cloth on my head when I'd've killed you dead and tossed you off a cliff."

"Don't want you dead," Arlen said. "You can still sit a horse with that splint. You go back peaceful, and I'll tell Malcum just enough so your license is all you lose."

Sandar barked a laugh. "Ent Malcum I'm worried about, it's Count Brayan. He gets wind I tried to rob him, and my head'll be on a pike before the sun sets."

"If the shipment gets through, I'll see to it you keep your head," Arlen said.

"You'll forgive me if I don't trust that," Sandar said.

Arlen shrugged. "Try and kill me again tonight if you're up to it, but I warn you, I'm a light sleeper. Cross me again and I'll break enough bones so you never sit a horse again, then drag you up to Brayan's Gold with me to look the people you tried to rob in the eye."

Sandar nodded. "Sleep easy, I'll go back peaceful. Curk was right. You got a death wish, boy. Seen it before. Odds are you won't live long enough to tell anyone anything."

Arlen had already broken camp by the time the demons sank back down into the Core in the pre-dawn light. He and Sandar left the wardstone and parted ways as the sun crested the mountainside.

The temperature grew colder as he ascended the winding mountain path. Spring was on in full on the Milnese plain, but here patches of snow were still visible, and his armor no longer seemed so warm with the wind chilling the steel. He began walking for long periods each day, as much to keep his blood flowing as to take some of the load off Dawn Runner, valiantly doing the work of two horses. They moved slower as a result, but there were still hours left before dark when Arlen reached the next of Brayan's great wardposts. He kept on, and camped at dusk behind his own circles. The following day he came upon the next post early, and the fourth right at dusk, making camp in its shelter.

The trail grew steeper, trees turning stunted and vegetation sparse amidst the rock and snow. The trail meandered, the never-ending wagon ruts skirting for miles around obstacles that had been too great for the trailblazers to cut or dig through. But still they climbed, and the weather grew colder. The ruts became indentations in the snow, and the trees vanished entirely.

He ceased trying to pass Brayan's wardposts, so tired by day's end that he was glad of their protection, though he often had to sweep the snow from them to restore full potency.

On his seventh day out from Miln, Arlen spotted the waystation Malcum had promised, far up the slope. It was a small structure, barely a hut, but after days of freezing cold, biting wind, and loneliness, Arlen was more than ready for a night indoors with someone to talk to.

"Ay, the station!" he cried, his call echoing off the stone facing above.

"Ay, Messenger!" a call came echoing back a moment later.

It was still the better part of an hour before Arlen reached the station, built into the side of the mountain. The warding on the building wasn't elegant, but it was thorough, and contained many wards Arlen was not familiar with. He took out his journal to quickly sketch them.

The station keeper, a yellow-bearded man wrapped in a heavy jacket lined with nightwolf pelt and bearing Count Brayan's arms, came out to greet him. He was young, perhaps twenty winters, and carried no weapon. He strode right up to Arlen, extending a gloved hand to shake.

"You're not Sandar," he said, smiling.

"Sandar broke his leg," Arlen said.

"There's a Creator, after all," the man laughed. "I'm Derek of the Goldmen."

"Arlen Bales of Tibbet's Brook," Arlen replied, gripping the hand firmly.

"So you know what it's like to live at the end of the world," Derek said. "I want to hear all about it." He clapped Arlen's shoulder. "Coffee's hot inside, if you want to go warm up. I'll stable your horse and stow the cart." It was only midday, but there was no question that Arlen would stay the night. Derek seemed as desperate for someone to talk to as Arlen.

"I'm warm enough to see the cargo stowed." Arlen

said, though his feet and hands ached from the cold, and he could no longer feel his face. After what happened with Sandar, he didn't intend to let the crates of thundersticks out of his sight until they were under lock and key.

Derek shrugged. "You're free to suffer as you like." He took Dawn Runner's bridle and led the way to a pair of wooden barn doors embedded in the rock face of the mountain.

"Quickly, now," Derek said, as he grasped the great iron ring hanging from one of the doors, "don't want to let the heat escape." He opened the door just enough to admit the cart, and Arlen quickly led Dawn Runner through. There was a moment of sweet warmth, but then an icy wind roared in through the door as Derek was pulling it shut behind them, stealing the comfort.

Shivering, Arlen found himself in a small chamber, walled at the far end with a curtain of thick, ragged furs. Oil lamps flickered on either wall.

Derek took a lamp and drew the curtain aside to allow them passage. Arlen gaped. The entryway was just an alcove at the far end of a vast chamber, cut deep into the mountainside. It was filled with pens to handle teams of animals, granaries for their feed, and stowing area for a dozen carts. It was mostly empty now, but Arlen could well imagine the bustle and energy that ran through this great room when a caravan was passing though.

By the time the cart and horse were stowed, Arlen was sweating in his armor again. He looked about the great chamber, but there was no sign of a furnace vent or fire.

"Why's it so warm in here?" he asked.

Derek led him to the stone wall and knelt, pointing to a swirling pattern of wards painted at about knee height along the wall in either direction.

Arlen studied the pattern. It wasn't complex, but it was brilliant. "Heat wards. So the corelings attack the station doors outside . . ."

"And their magic gets leached in here to warm the walls," Derek finished. "Some nights it gets hot as firespit, though. Almost rather be cold." Arlen, stifling in his armor, understood completely.

They took a side door out of the chamber and into the station itself. The ceiling, walls, and floor were the living stone of the mountain, cut into long halls, doorways, and chambers. Heat wards ran along the base of the walls here, too.

"Didn't realize the station went back so far into the mountain," Arlen said.

"Nowhere else to go without blocking the road, and that's narrow enough," Derek said. "That pine lodge is just the front porch. Come on, I'll show you your chamber."

"Thanks," Arlen said. "If I don't get out of this ripping armor soon, I'm going to melt. Been sleeping in it a week now."

"Smells like it," Derek said. "You can have the royal chamber, seeing as how there's no one else here to take it. There's a tub."

The royal chamber was meant to allow Count Brayan and his heirs the luxury they were accustomed to when they went to inspect the mines. The chamber was very fine, filled with oak furniture, fur rugs, and heat-warded stones. Most importantly, there was a proper bed, with a feathered mattress.

"The sun shines at last," Arlen said.

"Tub's over there," Derek said, pointing to a smooth depression in the stone floor beneath a heavy pump. "Pump's attached to a heated reservoir. Soak as long as you like and then come out for supper."

Arlen nodded, and the keeper left. He meant to take his armor off and get in the bath, but he fell back on the mattress for a moment, savoring its soft support, and found he didn't have the strength to rise. He closed his eyes, and fell dead asleep.

Arlen eventually made it out of his armor and over to the bath. Working the pump to fill the tub woke him back up, but the hot soak threatened to put him right out again. It was only the insistent growl of his stomach that made him pull on his clothes and stumble out of his room, feeling practically weightless without his armor.

"Derek?" he called.

"In the kitchen!" he heard the keeper reply. "Follow your nose!"

Arlen sniffed the air, and the growl in his stomach became a roar. His nose led him swiftly to the kitchen, where he found Derek wearing an apron and thick leather gloves as he bustled about.

"Sit," the keeper told Arlen, pointing to the closest stool at an oval table at the room's center, large enough for a score of men to eat at once. "Supper will be ready in a moment. You feeling human again?"

Arlen nodded as he sat. "It's only now that I'm clean, I realize just how filthy I was."

Derek went to a keg, filling a mug with foaming ale. He slid it across the polished table to Arlen with practiced ease. "Keep the kegs out in the snow till they're needed. Tapped this one special for you." He took his own mug and raised it in toast.

Arlen raised his in reply, and they both drank deeply. He looked at his cup in sudden surprise. "Might be a week on the road talking, but I'd swear that's Boggin's Ale."

"All the way from Tibbet's Brook," Derek agreed, taking Arlen's mug and putting a fresh head on it. "There are benefits to knowing every Messenger, wagon driver, and caravan guard by name."

"Boggin's was the first ale I ever drank," Arlen said, taking another swallow and letting it slide slowly over his tongue. Suddenly, he was twelve years old again, listening to Ragen and Old Hog haggling at the General Store in Tibbet's Brook.

"Nothing's better than your first," Derek said.

Arlen nodded, drinking again. "My life changed forever that day."

Derek laughed. "You and every other man." He set his mug down to take hollowed loaves of hard bread and fill them with a thick meat and vegetable stew.

Arlen fell on the meal like a coreling, tearing chunks of the warm crust and using them to scoop the delicious stew into his mouth. In minutes, he had scraped the plate clean down to the last crumb and speck of gravy. No meal in his life had ever been so satisfying.

"Night, even my mam never cooked like that," he said.

Derek smiled. "Ent got much else to do out here, so I've become a fair hand in the kitchen." He cleared the plates and ale mugs, replacing them with coffee cups. The brew smelled amazing.

"We can take the coffee out on the porch and watch the sunset, if you like," Derek said. "Got big windows made of that new warded glass they started making a couple years ago. You ever seen that?"

Arlen smiled. He was the one who had brought the glass wards to Miln, and Cob's shop did all Count Brayan's glasswork. He had probably warded the panes himself.

"I've heard of it," he said, not wanting to deflate the keeper, who looked quite proud.

As they left the kitchen, the stone floor became smooth pine boards, and they came to a large common area with fine pillowed benches and low tables.

Arlen's eyes were immediately drawn to the window, and he gasped.

He had once thought the view of the mountains from the roof of the Duke's Library in Miln was the grandest in the world, but it was only a fraction of the view from the waystation, which seemed to tower over the mountains themselves. Far below, clouds swirled, and when they parted, he could see the tiny speck of Fort Miln, far, far below.

They sat by the windows, and Derek produced a pair of pipes and a weed pouch, along with a drybox of matches. For a short while, they smoked and drank their coffee in silence, watching the sun set from the top of the world.

"Don't think I've ever seen anything so beautiful," Arlen said.

Derek sighed, sipping his coffee. "Used to think so, too, but now it's just the fourth wall of my prison."

Arlen looked at him, and Derek blushed. "Sorry. Don't mean to steal the sight from you."

Arlen waved the thought away. "Honest word, I know how you feel. How often do they relieve you?"

"Used to be one month off and one on," Derek said, "but then I got caught in an abandoned shaft with the Baron's daughter over the winter, and he nearly had my stones cut off. Said he'd be corespawned before his daughter married a Servant. Been stuck out here three months now with no relief. Reckon she must've bled by now, else they would've called me back and fetched a Tender. I'll be lucky if they let me come home when the station closes for the winter."

"You've been alone here for three months?" Arlen asked. The thought was maddening.

"Mostly," the keeper said. "Messenger comes every fortnight, give or take, and caravans come a few times a year. Weeks on my arse, and then suddenly I've got a dozen wagons and fifty head of cattle and pack animals to manage, along with thirty guards needing quarter and a Royal to shout at me as I tend them."

"Was she worth it?" Arlen asked.

Derek chuckled. "Stasy Talor? Ent no girl in the world finer, and you can tell her I said so. I could just as easily have ended up the Baron's son-in-law instead of exiled out here."

"Can't you quit?" Arlen asked. "Find some other work?"

Derek shook his head. "There's only one work in Brayan's Gold, and that's what the baron gives you. If he says spend all year at the waystation, well . . ." He shrugged. "Still, I reckon talking to myself all day is better than swinging a pick in a dark mine shaft, worrying about cave-ins or digging too deep and opening a path to the Core."

"I don't think it works that way," Arlen said.

"Looks safer than Messaging, too," Derek said. "What happened to your cheek?"

Arlen reached up on reflex, running his fingers lightly over the wound where the bandit's arrow had pierced his cheek. He had treated it with herbs before stitching and it was healing well enough, but the flesh around the wound was an angry red and crusted with blood, obvious to anyone at a glance.

"Got hit by bandits after the thundersticks," he said. "Just past the third caravan wardpost." He quickly told the tale.

Derek grunted. "You got stones like a rock demon, waving a thunderstick around like that. Lucky they weren't looking to hurt anyone. A bad winter can put some folk past caring."

Arlen shrugged. "I wasn't giving up the cargo on my first real Messenger run without a fight. Sets a bad precedent."

Derek nodded. "Well, you ent likely to find any bandits the rest of the way. You'll be in Brayan's Gold the evening after next."

"Why so long?" Arlen said. "Aren't we almost at the top? Figure I can crack the whip and make it the rest of the way before late afternoon."

Derek laughed. "Air gets thin up there, Messenger. Just going up the cart path will have you laboring for breath like you were scaling the rock face. Even I feel tired for a couple of days when I go home, and I was born there."

By then, the sun was only a thin line of fire on the horizon, and a moment later, it winked out, leaving them in near-darkness for the rising. Outside, the whiteness of the snow resisted the darkening sky.

Arlen turned to Derek, who was little more than a silhouette. The bowl of his pipe glowed softly as he pulled at it. "Aren't you going to light any lamps?"

Derek shook his head. "Just wait."

Arlen shrugged and turned his attention back to the window, watching a rock demon rise on the road outside. It was the same slate color as those lower on the mountain, but smaller still, with long, spindly arms and legs with two joints. Sharp bits of horn jutted along its limbs, and it walked as much on all fours as it did upright.

"Always expected rock demons got bigger, the higher up you go," Arlen said. "Don't know why."

"Opposite's true," Derek said. "Less to hunt up here, and the deep snow trips up the big ones."

"That's good to know," Arlen said.

The rock demon caught sight of them and launched itself at the window with frightening speed. Arlen had never seen a rock move so fast or leap so far. It struck the wardnet in midair, and magic flared like lightning, throwing the demon back onto the road and almost pitching it down the mountainside. The coreling caught itself just in time, long talons catching fast in the rock at the cliff's edge.

Suddenly, all the wards at the front of the station came to life, flaring in succession as the magic leached from the rock demon activated the wardnet, the pattern of symbols dancing across the walls and beams.

Many of the wards winked out soon after flaring,

but Arlen could feel the heat wards still radiating faintly, and interspersed through the net and room were light wards, glowing with a soft, lingering luminescence.

Another coreling came at the window, a wind demon that shrieked as it dove from the sky. The net flared again, and the heat wards grew warmer as the light wards grew brighter. More corelings came at the window, and within a few minutes, the room was brighter than a dozen lamps might have made it, and warmer than if it had a roaring fire.

"Amazing," Arlen said. "I've never seen warding like this."

"Count Brayan spares no expense on his own comfort," Derek said. A demon suddenly struck the wards right in front of him, and he jumped, then scowled and made an obscene gesture at the offending demon.

"They always come at the window," Derek said. "Same demons, every night. I keep thinking one night they'll just give up, but they never learn."

"Seeing you makes them crazed," Arlen said. "Corelings might eat what they kill, but I think it's the kill itself that feeds them, human kills most of all. If they know you're here, they'll come and test the wards every night, even if it takes a hundred years for one to fail."

"Night, that's no comfort," Derek said.

"We're not meant to be comfortable, so long as night

reigns," Arlen said, looking back out the window. "Is it just rock and wind demons up this high, then?"

"And snow demons," Derek said. "They rise even higher, where the snow never melts, but they'll drift down in a winter storm."

"You've seen snow demons?" Arlen asked, gaping at him.

"Oh, sure," Derek said, but under Arlen's glare, his expression grew less confident. "Once," he amended. "I think."

"You think?" Arlen asked.

"Window was foggy from the heat wards," Derek admitted.

Arlen raised an eyebrow, but Derek only shrugged. "I'm not looking to spin you some ale story. Maybe I saw one, maybe I didn't. Don't matter. I ent gonna stop drawing the wards. Jongleurs say that's what did us in, the first time. I'll keep drawing wards even if I never see a coreling again so long as I live. Tell my kids and grandkids to do the same."

"Honest word," Arlen agreed. "Will you teach me the snow wards?"

"Ay, I've some slate and chalk over there," Derek said, pointing. He tapped out his pipe as Arlen fetched the items, handing them to Derek and looking on eagerly as he drew.

He was surprised to see that the basic ward of forbidding for snow demons was an alteration of the water demon ward—lines flowing out to make the ward look almost like a snowflake. Derek continued to draw, and Arlen, a skilled Warder, quickly saw how the energy would move through the net. His hand moved of its own accord, inscribing perfect copies and notes in his journal.

Arlen was back in the feathered bed when One Arm tracked him to the station. He heard the demon's keening clearly, and the thunderous cracks as it tested the wards. The station was well protected, but with the giant rock demon powering the heat and light wards, the room grew continually hotter and brighter until it seemed he was standing in the sun at noon on a cloudless summer day in Soggy Marsh. Arlen lay bathed in sweat, the steam filtering in from the yard, making everything damp. He would be sanding rust from his armor for days when he got home.

Finally, when sleep seemed impossible, he got up and began inscribing Derek's snow wards into his portable circles until morning. Derek was unable to sleep either, and had the cart hitched and ready to go. Arlen was on his way the moment the sun touched the mountainside.

As the keeper had warned, the going was much harder now. The cold of the road was welcome at first after the stifling heat of the station, but it wasn't long before the chill crept back into his bones, especially with his cloak and underclothes damp. An icy rime soon built up on his breastplate, and try as he might, Arlen could not seem to draw a full breath. Even

Dawn Runner wheezed and gasped. They moved at a crawl, and though it had only been a few miles, they came to the next wardpost late in the day. Arlen had no desire to press on further.

The next day was harder still. His lungs had started to grow accustomed to the altitude overnight, but the trail continued to climb.

"There must be a lot of gold up there," Arlen told Dawn Runner, "to make this trip worth it." He immediately regretted the statement, not for lack of truth, but because the simple act of speaking aloud burned his lungs.

There was nothing for it but to press on, so Arlen put his head down and ignored the biting wind and drifts of powdery snow that came up to his knees in places. The wagon ruts vanished and the trail became all but invisible, though markers were hardly needed. There was only one passable direction, bounded by the mountainside and a sheer cliff.

By afternoon, Arlen's entire body burned for lack of air, and the weight of his armor was unbearable. He would have taken it off, but he feared that if he stopped to do so, he might never get his legs to start walking again.

Plenty of folk make this trip, he reminded himself. *Ent nothing they did you can't do too.*

It was late in the day, with both Arlen and Dawn Runner on their last legs, when the small mining town came into sight. Brayan's Gold was a mixture of semi-permanent structures, some of wood, and others built from the detritus of the mines, packed dirt, and cut or pulverized stone. Most of the structures were poor, having tanned skins for doors and extensions made from tents, but there was a great wooden inn at the town's center, dominating the plateau.

Some few people moved about, women and children mostly, the men likely at work in the mines. Arlen wet his dry and cracked lips, putting his Messenger horn to them and blowing a long, clear note. The act sent knives of ice down his throat.

"Messenger!" a boy called. A moment later, Arlen was surrounded by children, jumping up and down and asking what he had brought them.

Arlen smiled. He had done the same when he was a boy and the Messenger came to Tibbet's Brook. He'd come prepared, and tossed sugar candies wrapped in twists of corn husk, small toys, and puzzles to the children. Their joy washed over him like a hot bath. Suddenly, climbing the mountain did not seem such an ordeal, and he found some of his strength returning.

"I want to be a Messenger some day," a boy declared, and Arlen ruffled his hair, slipping him an extra candy.

"You're a day early," someone said, and Arlen turned to see a small man dressed in a fine wool coat, his suede boots and gloves trimmed in white ermine fur. Behind him were two burly guards with small pick mattocks hanging from their belts that looked as much weapon as tool. The man approached with a genial smile, extending his hand.

"Ran into some bandits," Arlen said, shaking the hand. "Pressed ahead and skipped a wardpost to get some distance."

"Talor," the man introduced himself, "Count Brayan's cousin, and Baron of Brayan's Gold. What happened to Sandar?"

"Broke his leg," Arlen said. "I'm Arlen Bales."

Talor put his hand on Arlen's shoulder, leaning in close. "I'll tell you the same three things I tell every Messenger on his first run here: The climb is always hardest the first time, you'll catch your breath by morning, and it's easier going down than coming up." He laughed as if it were some great joke and slapped the back of Arlen's armor with a clank.

"Still, I'm surprised they sent a first-timer here alone," Talor said.

"Had Messenger Curk with me, but he turned tail when the bandits hit," Arlen said.

Talor's eyes narrowed. "The shipment is intact?"

Arlen smiled. "Down to the last crate-nail." He handed over a wax-sealed tube pressed with Count Brayan's pick and hammer sigil as well as Curk's and his own seals.

"Ha!" the baron barked, his sudden tension gone. He slapped Arlen hard on the back. "This sounds like a tale for inside where it's warm!"

Talor raised a hand and his guards took the cart.

Arlen walked beside him as he popped the seal on the tube and took out the manifest, his eyes running across the lines listing every item on the cart, down to the last letter and personal package. There was a personal letter from the count included in the tube, but Arlen was not privy to its contents. The baron stuffed the unopened envelope in his jacket pocket.

They came to the stable, where boys were unhitching Dawn Runner as the guards unloaded the cart. Arlen moved to help, but Talor put out a hand to hold him back.

"You just spent a week and more on the road, Messenger. Let the Servants handle the back bending." He handed the manifest to one of the stable guards and led the way inside.

Like the waystation, the inside of the inn was heat warded and quite warm. At its front was a general store, the only resource in town for the necessities of life. Shelves behind the counter were filled with various tools and implements on sale, and chalked slates listed prices for food, livestock, and specialty items.

The room was crowded with women, many with children at their skirts as they called to the women taking orders and coin at the counter, who then called stocking instruction to more of Baron Talor's burly guards.

After the silence of the road, the din was overwhelming, but the baron quickly led the way through to the taproom in back and a quiet alcove with a richly appointed table. The bartender immediately brought them coffee.

Arlen blew on his steaming cup and sipped, the warmth beginning to seep back into his bones. The baron gave him time to take his ease until two women approached the table, one young, and another much older. Their dresses were plainer than Royal ladies favored in Fort Miln, but the fine cut and cloth still marked them.

Arlen stood politely as the baron kissed the women and turned to make introductions. "Messenger Arlen Bales, may I present my wife, Lady Delia Talor, and my daughter, Stasy."

Arlen noted the lack of the title "Mother" before the baroness' name, but he made no comment, bowing and kissing hands just as Cob had taught him.

The baroness was in her late fifties and no beauty, with a pinched face and a long neck, making her seem like a fishing bird. Stasy Talor, however, was all that Derek had claimed.

She was of an age with Arlen, with dark hair and blue eyes, tall and lithe in the Milnese way. She was pretty of face, but Arlen thought it was the sad cast to her eyes that made her truly beautiful. The lacings of her bodice were undone, as if the dress no longer fit well.

Reckon she must've bled by now, Derek had said, but suddenly Arlen wasn't so sure. He had to force his eyes up to meet hers before he was caught staring.

They all sat, and the baron and baroness leaned in close as they broke the seal and read Count Brayan's private letter. They began whispering harshly to one another and glancing at Stasy, but Arlen affected not to notice. He turned to the girl, hoping to engage her in conversation, but the baron's daughter did not acknowledge him, watching the discussion with her sad eyes.

Finally, the baron grunted and turned back to Arlen. "We'll soon be sending a caravan to Miln, so you can leave the cart here and head back with your horse alone. There will only be a handful of letters for your return."

Arlen nodded, and soon after a rich lunch was served. The baron and his wife kept up a constant flow of questions, asking for news from Miln, and Arlen dutifully recited every going on of note in the great city, along with whatever gossip he had overheard around the Messengers' Guildhouse. It was the gossip the Royals in exile seemed to covet most of all. Stasy took no part in the conversation, her eyes on her lap.

At last, a guard came over to the table with a chalked slate and the manifest. "There's a thunderstick missing." He eyed Arlen suspiciously.

"Nonsense," Talor said. "Count them again."

"Counted twice," the guard said.

The baron scowled, and his eyes flicked to Arlen for just an instant. His smile was forced. "Count a third time," he told the guard.

Arlen cleared his throat. "No, he's right. The missing stick's in front, tucked under the seat. I used it to scare my way past the bandits." He tried to tell himself he had forgotten the stick was there, but he knew deep down that he had left it there on purpose, hoping that perhaps no one would notice it was missing from the crate.

Everyone looked at him in shock. Even Stasy's eyes came up. Arlen quickly explained his encounter with the bandits, though he made no mention of Sandar.

Still, Baron Talor's mouth fell open with the telling. "You bluffed your way through by waving a thunderstick?"

Arlen smiled. "Never said I was bluffing."

Talor barked a laugh, and shook his head. "Not sure if that's the bravest or the craziest thing I ever heard! If it's true, you've got stones like a rock demon."

"They say a man doesn't become a Messenger unless he does," the baroness purred, giving Arlen a look that made him shudder. "But how did they find out about the shipment? Only Mother Cera and I knew the exact date."

"And Sandar," Arlen said, "who supposedly broke his leg the morning of."

"That's a big accusation, Messenger," Talor said, a quiet danger to his voice. "Have you any proof?"

Arlen knew his next words could mean life or death for Sandar. He shrugged. "Not accusing anybody.

I'm just saying that if I was you, I'd get myself a new Messenger."

"How do we know you aren't just trying to get the job yourself?" the baroness asked.

"I'm just an apprentice," Arlen said. "Guild won't give me the job regardless."

"Bah." The baroness waved dismissively. "We could change that with a flick of a pen, and you know it. If you're telling the truth, we owe you a great debt."

Arlen nodded. "'Preciate that, milady, but I got an eye to see the world a bit before I settle on a regular run."

The baroness tsked. "You young ones always do, but one day you may not think steady work on a familiar path such a bad thing."

After lunch, the baron and the baroness stood. Arlen quickly got to his feet as well, and Stasy followed, her eyes still hollow.

"You'll have to excuse us," Talor said, "but we have some business to attend. Stasy will see you assigned a room and have the boys prepare supplies for your return. Compliments of Count Brayan, of course."

They vanished in a swirl of expensive fur, and Stasy gave a shallow curtsey. "Daughter Stasy, to serve you," she mumbled.

"You make it sound like a death sentence," Arlen said.

Finally, the baron's daughter met his eyes. "I apologize, Messenger, but the letter you brought from the count may as well have been." Her tone was the resigned one of someone whose tears are long dried.

"My legs still ache from the climb," Arlen said, gesturing to the table. "Will you sit with me a little longer?"

Stasy nodded and allowed Arlen to pull her chair. "As you wish."

Taking his own seat across from her, Arlen leaned over the table, his voice low. "They say if you whisper a secret to a Messenger, it's safer than a Tender's ear. No man, nor all the demons of the Core, can pull it unwilling from his lips, save the one it's meant for."

"This from the man who spread court gossip to my parents for the last hour," Stasy noted.

Arlen smiled. "Once those rumors reach the main hall of the Messengers' Guild, they are no longer secret, but I will tell you something that is."

Stasy raised an eyebrow. "Oh?"

"Derek still thinks there ent no woman finer than Stasy Talor, and prays you haven't bled," Arlen said. "Said I could tell you so."

Stasy gasped and put a hand to her chest. Her pale cheeks turned bright red and she looked around guiltily, but there was no one to see. She met his eyes fully now.

"Clearly I haven't," she said, absently touching the loose lacing about her belly. "But it makes no difference. He is not good enough for me."

"Are those your words, or your father's?" Arlen asked.

Stasy shrugged. "What does it matter? My father might have taken the 'i' from his name when Mother died and he married Count Brayan's Royal cousin, but amongst the other nobles, he still feels like a Merchant, because his access to Royal circles is only as strong as his marriage vows. He wants better for me, and that means bearing children to a proper Royal husband and attending the Mothers School."

Arlen resisted the urge to spit on the floor. His father had tried to force him into an arranged marriage when he was eleven, and he remembered how it felt.

"Ent got anyone calling themselves Royal where I come from," he said. "Reckon we're better for it."

"Honest word," Stasy agreed sadly.

"How will your father arrange that, once your state is known?" Arlen asked.

Stasy laughed mirthlessly. "Likely he won't be able to, which is why that 'caravan' he's sending will ship me off to Count Brayan's Court to have my babe in secret amongst the Servants, at which point Countess Mother Cera will present me at court as having just arrived in the city and broker me a 'proper' marriage. Derek will never even know he's a father."

"You'll have to pass the waystation," Arlen said.

"Won't matter," Stasy said. "A new keeper will be sent with us to relieve him, and he'll be on his way back up the mountain before he even knows I'm locked in the coach."

She looked around to make sure they were not being

watched, then reached out and gripped Arlen's hand. He saw passion in her eyes, and a thirst for adventure. "But if Derek knew what was coming and had supplies hidden, he could sneak down the mountain instead of up. Even if Father sent someone after us the moment Derek went missing, we'd have a week's lead. More than enough to find each other, sell my jewelry, and disappear into the city. We could get married no matter what his station and raise our child together."

Stasy looked at him, her eyes burning. "If you'll tell him this, Messenger, with no word to any other or mark in your log, I will pay whatever you ask."

Arlen looked at her, feeling as protective as an elder brother. He would take her message for nothing, but he could not deny there was something he wanted. Something the baron's daughter might be able to arrange.

"I need a thunderstick," he said quietly.

Stasy snorted. "Is that all? I'll have half a dozen of them packed with your supplies."

Arlen gaped, shocked at how easy it had been, but it quickly melted into a smile.

"What do you need the stick for?" Stasy asked.

"Gonna kill a rock demon that's been following me," Arlen said.

Stasy tilted her head, studying him in that way people had, as if trying to determine if he were joking or simply mad. At last she gave a slight shrug and met his eyes. "Just promise you'll deliver my message first."

Arlen took an extra couple of days to catch his breath while the Goldmen finished preparing their messages for his return trip. He still tired easily in the thin mountain air, but the effects bothered him less each day. He spent the time wisely, watching the miners put the new thundersticks to use. Everyone wanted the favor of the new Messenger, so they were quick to answer his questions.

After watching as they reduced a solid rock face into tons of rubble in an ear-splitting instant, Arlen knew the destructive power of the thunderstick had not been exaggerated. If anything in the world could penetrate One Arm's thick carapace, it was this.

At last all was in order, and on the third day he put his heavy armor back on and headed to the stables. His saddlebags were already packed with supplies, and in them, Arlen found a small box of thundersticks packed in straw, along with a sealed envelope addressed to Derek in flowing script.

As the Baron had promised, it was far easier going down the trail than coming up. He made it to the first wardpost early in the day and pressed on, making the station well before dusk. Derek came out to meet him.

"I've a special letter for you," Arlen said, handing him the envelope. The keeper's eyes lit up at the sight, and he held the unopened letter up to the sun.

"Creator," he prayed, "please let it be that she ent bled."

He tore the letter open excitedly, but as he read

his smile faded and his face slowly drained of color, becoming as white as the snow around him. He looked up at Arlen in horror.

"Night," he said. "She's out of her corespawned mind. Does she honestly think I'm going to run off to Miln?"

"Why wouldn't you?" Arlen asked. "You just prayed to the Creator for this very thing."

"Sure, when I thought it would make me the Baron's son-in-law, not when it means a week and more alone with the corelings."

"What of it?" Arlen asked. "There're campsites the whole way, and you're a fine Warder."

"You know what the worst thing about being a keeper is, Messenger?" Derek asked.

"Loneliness?"

Derek shook his head. "It's that one night it takes to get home. Sure, you can tumble downhill to the station in a day, but going back up, you always have to stop at that corespawned wardpost." He shuddered. "Watching the corelings stalk with nothing between you but magic. Don't know how you Messengers do it. I always come home with piss frozen to my breeches. I ent ever even done it alone. My da and brothers always come out when I'm relieved, so the four of us can take turns at watch."

"Folk make the trip all the time," Arlen said.

"And every year, at least half a dozen of them are cored on the way," Derek said. "Sometimes more."

"Careless people," Arlen said.

"Or just unlucky," Derek said. "Ent no girl worth that. I like Stasy well enough, and she's a ripping good rut if you get her alone, but she ent the only girl in Brayan's Gold."

Arlen scowled. Derek's calm obstinance, producing excuse after excuse for his cowardice, reminded him of his father. Jeph Bales, too, had turned his back on wife and child when it meant spending a night out of walls, and it had cost Arlen's mother her life.

"You go back to Brayan's Gold without Stasy and your child, you ent half a man," he said, and spit on the ground.

Derek growled and balled a fist. "What's it to you anyway, Messenger? What do you care if I run off with the Baron's daughter or not?"

"I care because that girl and the babe she's carrying deserve better than a ripping coward," Arlen said, and then there was a flash behind his eyes as Derek punched him.

He rolled with the blow, coming around to drive his steel-plated elbow hard into the keeper's kidney.

Derek howled and doubled over, and Arlen's next swing took him full in the face, laying him out flat in the snow.

Feelings long buried came roaring to the surface, and Arlen had to check himself against a desire to continue the beating. He got back on his horse.

"Don't think I'll be staying," he told Derek as the

keeper rolled up onto his elbow, shaking his head to clear it. "Rather spend a night alone with the corelings than behind warded walls with a man who'll turn his back on his own child."

The trail climbed a ridge and then dropped steeply, leaving Brayan's Gold and the waystation on the far side of the mountain. Arlen's bruised cheek throbbed dully in the cold, and his mood grew blacker as he went. It was not the first time he had underestimated a man and felt betrayed, nor would it likely be the last, but always it was for the same reason. Fear. Fear of the corelings. Fear of the night. Fear of death.

Fear's a good thing, his father used to say. *It keeps us alive.*

But as with so many things, his father had been wrong. Jeph Bales had taken his fear and embraced it so fully he was convinced it was wisdom. Allowing himself to be ruled by fear might have extended Jeph's years, but under its heavy yoke, Arlen doubted his father had ever truly lived.

I will respect the corelings, Arlen thought, *but I will never stop fighting them.*

An hour before sunset, he stopped and made camp, laying out his circles and hobbling Dawn Runner, making sure she was well blanketed. He glanced at the crate of thundersticks, and decided he could wait no longer. Not far back, he had crossed a narrow pass that was perfect for his purposes. He took two spears, two thundersticks, and his shield, hiking back uphill. He soon found the pass, overlooked by an escarpment much like the spot Sandar had chosen to waylay him and Curk.

He headed up the trail a bit farther, scattering small lacquered plates etched with light wards in the snow along the path One Arm was soon to come bounding down. He returned to the pass and climbed the escarpment, looking out eagerly over the trail as he waited for dusk.

Twilight came quickly, and the stench of the demons rose with their foul mist, seeping from the ground to pollute the surface. The demons were sparse here, but not three feet from Arlen, a rock demon began to form on the escarpment, a squat beast, with armor the same color as the stone.

Arlen knew the demon would not notice him until it was fully formed, but he did not run or prepare a circle. Instead he crouched, waiting for the demon to solidify. When it was fully opaque, he rushed in, shield leading. There was a full elemental circle of protection etched around the shield's edge, and magic flared as Arlen reached the coreling, stopping him short and hurling the rock demon off the outcropping, clear over the side of the cliff face.

Arlen smiled as the demon's roar receded to a distant crashing. There was a crack, and a shelf of snow far below broke free, burying the coreling where it landed. He doubted a fall could ever do lasting harm to a rock demon, but he took pleasure in its rage all the same.

It was a clear night, and twilight gave way to moon and stars that cast a dim glow on the snow. Even so, he heard the distant rumble of One Arm's approach long before he caught sight of the giant rock demon.

He waited, match held in his shield hand and thunderstick in the other. His spears were stuck point-down in the snow, in easy reach. When the ward plates on the trail flared, filling the pass with light, Arlen struck his thumbnail against the match tip, lighting it with a pop. He touched the fuse of the thunderstick to the fire where it caught with a crackle. Immediately, he drew back his arm and threw, raising his shield and peeking over its edge.

One Arm stopped its charge, looking at the projectile curiously, but then its good arm whipped across, faster than Arlen would have imagined possible, to bat the stick away. It flew up out of sight before exploding with a force that shook the whole mountainside and knocked Arlen to one knee, his ears ringing. The bang echoed in the distance. One Arm was distracted for a moment, but seemed otherwise unaffected.

"Corespawn it," Arlen muttered as the giant demon turned its attention back toward him. He was thankful he had brought a spare.

Pulling out the second thunderstick, Arlen fumbled for a match as One Arm charged. He managed to light and throw the second stick, but again One Arm was quick, stopping short and this time catching the stick, pulling it in for a closer look.

Arlen ducked behind his shield as the thunderstick went off right in the demon's face. The night lit up with a roar, and the shockwave of heat and force bowled him over, nearly knocking Arlen from the escarpment. He fell flat and held on for dear life.

A moment later he laughed out loud and looked up, expecting to see half the demon's head blown off, but One Arm stood there unharmed.

"No!" Arlen screamed, as the demon roared and resumed its charge. "No! No! No!"

He took up one of his spears, drawing back and throwing hard. The missile struck the demon full in the chest, splintering on impact and doing no harm.

"What does it take to kill you?" Arlen cried, but the demon took no heed. Knowing the fight was lost, he cursed and dropped his shield to the ground, standing at the center of its small circle of protection.

But the ground shook from the demon's charge, a sound like constant thunder in the air, and Arlen's knees buckled. He stumbled from his perch atop the convex shield, and knew he could not trust its protection through the night.

Quickly, he picked his shield back up, taking a spear in his other hand. His armor might protect him long enough to retreat back to Dawn Runner's circle, but it was a long way to run through the snow at night, especially with seventy pounds of steel on his back. The roaring filled his ears, and it seemed the whole mountain shook.

One Arm reached the outcropping, leaping up to catch its lip. The great talons of its good arm dug into the stone as it pulled itself up. Arlen stabbed at the hand uselessly as the roaring sound grew deafening, and suddenly he realized it wasn't One Arm causing it. He looked up and saw nothing but whiteness, rushing at him like water.

Barely thinking, Arlen leapt from the far side of the escarpment, half-sliding and half-tumbling down to the trail. Ignoring the sharp spikes of pain from the fall, he immediately fetched up against the mountainside and raised his shield.

Shaken loose by the thundersticks, the avalanche struck One Arm full on, knocking the giant demon over the cliff in much the same manner as Arlen had its smaller cousin. He saw the demon fall an instant before being buried himself.

There was surprising weight to the snow, and Arlen's arm threatened to buckle, but he succeeded in creating a pocket of shelter, and when the rumbling ceased, he was able to quickly dig himself out as the majority of the snow continued on down the mountainside.

He went over to the edge of the cliff, but there was no sign of One Arm in the darkness, nor sound of its cries. Arlen laughed again and pumped a fist into the air. Perhaps he had not been able to kill the demon, but he had faced it again and lived to tell the tale, and it might be days before One Arm found his trail again.

A low growl sounded off to the side, and the grin died on Arlen's face. The avalanche must have brought a demon down from higher up the mountain. His hand tightened on his spear, and he turned slowly, shield up.

The moon and stars were bright and reflected off the snow, casting a gray gloom through the darkness. At first he didn't see it, but as the coreling drew closer, the wards on his armor and shield began to draw upon its magic, glowing softly.

There was movement in the wardlight, and finally Arlen caught sight of it, a demon with pure white scales that glittered like snowflakes. It looked much like a flame demon, no bigger than a mid-size dog and crouched on all fours, with a long snout and horns that ran back flat over pointed ears and a long, corded neck.

On impulse, Arlen spat upon the demon, and was amazed to find the rumor was true. As his spittle struck the pure white scales, it froze and burst with a crack.

The snow demon's eyes narrowed, and its snout split wide in what might have been a smile. It made a horrid sound in its throat, and spat back at him.

Arlen managed to get his shield up in time, catching the spray. The surface turned white with rime, and his shield arm grew numb from the cold.

The demon leapt at him then, and his shield, made brittle by the coreling's coldspit, shattered on impact. Arlen was knocked onto his back in the snow, but managed to get a leg between the demon and himself, kicking it away. The snow demon was knocked to the cliff's edge, but dug in its front claws and held fast, back talons scrabbling for purchase. In a moment it would be back at him.

Arlen shook off the remains of his shield and charged the demon, spear leading. He meant to send it tumbling down to wherever One Arm had landed, but the coreling recovered faster than he anticipated. It tamped down and sprang to meet his charge.

Arlen spun his spear into a horizontal defense, but the coreling caught the shaft in its teeth and bit through the thick wood like it was a celery stalk. Arlen took the two halves and swung them like clubs to box the demon's ears, knocking it aside.

Before the demon could recover, he turned and ran. It was one thing to press an advantage when a demon was hanging by its claws, but another to fight one head on. There were no snow wards on his armor, and he had no defense against its coldspit.

The wards on his armor continued to glow softly, helping light his way, but also serving as a beacon to the snow demon and any other corelings that might be in the area. He stumbled through the snow, using the downward slope to add reckless speed to his flight.

But in the end, it was not enough. His legs sank into the loose snow, but the snow demon ran across its surface like a bug skating on water. He felt it hit his back, knocking the wind from him and bearing him to the ground.

Arlen rolled with the impact, shaking the demon off before it could find a seam in his armor, but he had barely rolled onto his back before it was upon him again. He put up his armored forearm to hold it back, and the demon caught the thick steel plate in its teeth and began to squeeze.

Metal squealed and bent, and though his arm was still numbed by the coldspit, Arlen howled in agony. The demon's talons raked at him, tearing easily through the steel mesh at his joints, and piercing the larger plates like blacksmith shears.

Arlen felt the cold claws pierce his flesh, like being stabbed with icicles, and screamed into the night. The demon thrashed its head from side to side, teeth still clamped, threatening to tear his arm clear out of the socket. Blood spattered his face from the injured limb.

But in that instant, sure of his own death, Arlen caught sight of the demon's bare belly, smooth like new snow, and saw a chance. With the fingers of his free hand he caught a swab of his own blood and reached out, drawing a crude heat ward on the snow demon's stomach.

Immediately, the ward flared, brighter and more

powerful than any he had seen at the station. Those wards were powered by feedback alone, but this ward drew on the coreling's dark magic directly. Arlen felt his face burn from its power.

The demon shrieked and let go its grip, and Arlen shoved it away. It landed on its back, and Arlen saw his blood ward blacken the white scales, then burst into a flame that consumed the demon like sunlight. He was left panting in the snow, bloodied and torn, but very much alive as he watched the thrashing snow demon immolated in fire.

He stumbled quickly back to the campsite, breathing a great sigh of relief when he was once again within the safety of his circles. He needed a prybar to get some of the pieces of his armor off, but there was no choice, as the twisted metal cut off his blood flow in more than one place, and cut into his skin in others. He lit the fire he had wisely laid in advance, and spent the rest of the night huddled by it, trying to restore feeling to his arm as he stitched his flesh.

Feeling slowly returned to his numb arm, bringing with it a maddening pain as if he had been burned. But through it all, he was smiling. He hadn't killed the demon he set out to, but he had killed one none-theless, and that was more than anyone he had ever known could claim. Arlen welcomed the pain, for it meant he was alive when he had no right to be.

Arlen led Dawn Runner down the steep trails

the next morning, happy to walk and keep his blood pumping. Late in the day, there came a cry behind him.

"Messenger!"

Arlen turned to see Derek running hard after him. He stopped and the keeper soon caught up, stumbling to a stop. Arlen caught him with his good arm and set him to hang on Dawn Runner's saddle, red-faced and panting. His eye was blue and swollen where Arlen had punched him.

"You're a long way from the station," Arlen said, when the keeper caught his breath.

"Whole mountain heard those thundersticks in the night, and the slide that followed," Derek said. "I took my skis and went looking for you."

"Why?" Arlen asked.

Derek shrugged. "Figured either you were dead, and I should try and send your bones to your mother, or alive, and needing some help. You ent my favorite person, Messenger, but anyone deserves that much."

"That would have taken you to the site of the avalanche, six hours back," Arlen said, "where you would have seen my tracks, and known I was all right. Why keep on?"

Derek looked at his feet. "I knew you were right yesterday, about me not standing by my own. I think that's what got me so mad. Then when I saw what was left of the demon you killed, it was like a kick in the stones. Dunno what came over me, I just kept on going while my nerve held. Figure the caravan will think I'm dead, but they'll still have to get Stasy out of Brayan's Gold before her belly swells. I'll go to Miln and wait for her."

Arlen smiled and clapped him on the shoulder.

Cob was berating one of the apprentices when Arlen returned to the shop. Arlen's master was always snappish when he was worried. He looked up at the door chime and saw Arlen standing there, Derek in tow. The irritation left his face, and the apprentice wisely used the distraction to vanish into the back room.

"You made it back," Cob grunted, heading to sit at his workbench without pausing for so much as a handshake.

Arlen nodded. "This is Derek, out of Brayan's Gold. He's got a steady warding hand, and could use some work."

"You're hired," Cob said, picking up his etching tool. He pointed his leathery chin at Arlen's left arm, missing its armor and bound in a sling.

"What happened?"

"You now know someone who's met a snow demon firsthand," Arlen said.

Cob shook his head and laughed aloud, bending over his work. "Should've known if they were out there, you'd find one," he muttered.

Introduction to
THE GREAT BAZAAR

Every novel is a learning process for the author, and
The Warded Man (aka *The Painted Man* in the UK)
was no different. It was a real challenge, keeping the
story moving along quickly with page-turning "what
happens next?" tension, despite the book being close
to 450 pages and spanning fourteen years in the lives
of three separate characters. Part of the process was
learning when, for the greater good, to cut out scenes
I'd already written (even when I loved them). A more
important part of it was learning to look ahead and
not write some of those scenes in the first place.

The Great Bazaar was one of the latter. It is essen-
tially chapter 16.5 of *The Warded Man*, taking place
during the three-year gap between Chapters 16 and
17, when Arlen is working as a Messenger traveling
throughout the Free Cities.

This was an exciting, adventure-filled period in Arlen's life, and a very fertile spawning ground for short stories about him traveling from town to town, touching the lives of different people living behind the wards.

Like Caine in *Kung Fu*.

I have a lot of story ideas for those three years, but there wasn't space to include all of them in *The Warded Man*, and even if there had been, it would have robbed Arlen's race towards destiny of all its immediacy. So I decided to skip those side stories and get to them some other time, putting Arlen, at the beginning of Chapter 17 (Ruins), at the end of a long series of adventures, lightly sketched for the reader, wherein he became worldly, and culminating in his finding the lost city of Anoch Sun, the next true turning point in his life.

Some of those adventures will be told in upcoming novels, but the tale of how Arlen found the lost city itself was too big and self-contained to fit in that format, and I am excited to be able to present it here.

The Great Bazaar shows everything I love about Arlen, and showcases one of my favorite supporting characters, Abban the *khaffit*, with his own point of view for the first time. Whether you are a new reader interested in an introduction to Arlen's world, or a fan of the series looking for an appetizer before the next book publishes, I think you'll enjoy it.

5

THE GREAT BAZAAR

328 AR

Sunlight was heavy in the desert. More than heat or brightness, it was an oppressive weight, and Arlen kept finding himself hunching over as if to yield before it.

He was riding through the outskirts of the Krasian Desert, where there was nothing but cracked flats of dry clay as far as the eye could see in any direction. Nothing to provide shade or reflect heat. Nothing to sustain life.

Nothing to make a sane person wander out here, Arlen scolded himself, nevertheless straightening his back in defiance of the sun. He had a thin white robe on over his clothes, the hood pulled low over his eyes, and a veil over his mouth and nose. The cloth reflected some of the light, but it seemed scant protection. He had even slung a white sheet over his horse, a bay courser named Dawn Runner.

The horse gave a dry cough, attempting to dislodge the ever-present dust from its throat.

"I'm thirsty too, Dawn," Arlen said, stroking the horse's neck, "but we've used our water ration for the morning, so there's nothing for it but to endure."

Arlen reached again for Abban's map. The compass slung around his neck told him that they were still headed due east, but there was no sign of the canyon. It should have come in sight a day ago, and harsh rationing or no, they would have to turn back to Fort Krasia in another day if they did not reach the river and find water.

Or you could spare yourself a day of thirst and turn back now, a voice in his head said.

The voice was always telling him to turn back. Arlen thought of it as his father, the lingering presence of a man he hadn't seen in close to a decade. Its words were always the stern-sounding bits of wisdom that his father had liked to impart. Jeph Bales had been a good man, and honest, but his stern wisdom had kept him from traveling more than a few hours from his home for his entire life.

Every day away from succor was another night spent outside with the corelings, and not even Arlen took that lightly, but he had a deep and driving need to see things that no other man had seen, to go places no other man had gone. He had been eleven when he ran away from home. Now he was twenty, and had seen more of the world than any but a handful of other men.

Like the parch in Arlen's throat, the voice was simply another thing to be endured. The demons had made the world small enough. He would not let some nagging voice make it even smaller.

This time he was seeking Baha kad'Everam, a Krasian hamlet whose name translated into "Bowl of Everam," which was the Krasian name for the Creator. Abban's maps said it rested in a natural bowl formed by a dry lakebed in a river canyon. The hamlet was renowned for its pottery, but the pottery merchants had stopped coming more than twenty years ago, and a *dal'Sharum* expedition had found the Bahavans taken by the night. No one had gone back there since.

"I was on that expedition," Abban had claimed. Arlen had looked at the fat merchant doubtfully.

"It's true," Abban said. "I was just a novice warrior carrying spears for the *dal'Sharum*, but I remember the trek well. There was no sign of the Bahavans, but the village was intact. The warriors cared nothing for pottery, and thought it dishonorable to loot. Even now, there is pottery left in the ruins, waiting for any with the courage to claim it." He had leaned in closely then. "The work of a Bahavan pottery master would sell for a premium in the bazaar," he said meaningfully.

And now, Arlen was in the middle of the desert, wondering if Abban had made the whole thing up.

He went on for hours more before he caught sight of a shadow creasing across the clay flats ahead of him. He could feel his heart thudding in his chest as Dawn Runner's plodding hooves slowly brought the canyon into view. Arlen breathed a sigh of relief, reminding himself that he ignored his father's voice for a reason. He turned his horse south; the bowl came into sight not long after.

Dawn Runner was grateful when they rode down into the bowl's shade. The hamlet's residents had apparently shared the sentiment, because they had built their homes into the ancient canyon walls, cutting deeply into the living clay and extending outward with adobe buildings indistinguishable in color from the canyon and invisible from any distance. A perfect camouflage from the wind demons that soared out over the flats in search of prey.

But despite this protection, the Bahavans had still died out. The river had gone dry, and sickness and thirst had left them vulnerable to the corelings. Perhaps a few had attempted the trek through the desert to Fort Krasia, but if so, they were never heard from again.

Arlen's initial high spirits fell with the realization that he was riding into a graveyard. Again. He drew wards of protection in the air as he passed the homes, calling out "Ay, Bahavans!" in the vain hope that some survivors might remain.

Only the sound of his own voice echoed back to him. The cloth that had served to block sun from windows and doorways, where it remained at all, was ragged and filthy, and the wards cut into the adobe were faded and worn from years of exposure to harsh desert wind and grit. The walls were scarred by demon claws. There were no survivors here.

There were demon pits dug in the center of the village to trap and hold corelings for the sun, and blockades running up the steep stone stairways that zigzagged in tiers up the canyon wall to link the buildings. They were hastily built defenses, put in place by the *dal'Sharum* not to defend the Bahavans, but rather to honor them. Baha kad'Everam had been a village of *khaffit*, men whose caste made them unworthy of the right to hold spears or enter into Heaven, but even such as they deserved hallowed ground to lay to rest, that their spirits might be reincarnated into a higher caste, if they were worthy.

And there was only one way the *dal'Sharum* hallowed ground. They stained it with their blood, and the black ichor that flowed through coreling veins. They called it *alagai'sharak*, meaning "demon war," and it was a battle waged every night in Fort Krasia, an eternal struggle that would go on until all the demons were dead, or there were no more men to fight them. The warriors had danced one night's *alagai'sharak* in Baha kad'Everam, to sanctify the Bahavans' graveyard.

Arlen rode around the blockades and down to the riverbed, a mighty channel that now held only a muddy, buggy trickle of water. Some thin vegetation clung stubbornly to the water's edge, but farther back the stalks of dead plants jutted, choked with dust and too dry to rot.

The water collected in a few small pools, brown and stinking. Arlen filtered it through charcoal and cloth, but still looked at the water doubtfully, and decided to boil it, as well. Dawn Runner nibbled at the bits of weed and prickly grass while he worked.

It was getting late in the day, and Arlen looked at the setting sun resentfully. "C'mon, boy," he told the horse. "Time to lock ourselves up for the night."

He led Dawn Runner back up the bank and into the main courtyard of the village. With little rain or erosion, the demon pits, twenty feet deep and ten feet in diameter, remained intact, but the wards that had been cut into the stones around them were dirty and faded. Any demon thrown into one of the pits now would likely climb right back out.

Still, the pits gave some security. Arlen set up his portable circles right between the adobe walls and one pit, limiting the path of approach to his camp.

Ten feet in diameter, Arlen's portable warding circles were composed of lacquered wooden plates connected by lengths of stout rope. Each plate was painted with ancient symbols of forbiddance, enough to shield him from every known breed of coreling.

He laid them out in precise fashion, ensuring that the wards lined up correctly to form a seamless net.

He drove a stake into the clay inside one circle and looped rope around Dawn Runner's legs, hobbling the horse and tying it to the stake with a complicated knot. If the horse struggled or tried to bolt when the demons came, the ropes would tighten and hold it in place, but Arlen could free the knot with but a tug, dropping the loops and freeing Dawn Runner instantly.

In the other circle, Arlen made his own camp. He laid a fire, but did not yet set spark to it, for wood was precious this far out, and the desert night would grow bitter cold.

As he worked, Arlen's eyes kept drifting up the stone steps to the adobe buildings built into the walls. Somewhere up there was the workshop of Master Dravazi, an artisan whose painted pottery had been worth its weight in gold while he lived, and was priceless now. One original Dravazi, lying forgotten on the potter's wheel, would likely finance his entire trip. More would make him a very rich man.

Arlen even had a good idea of where the master's workshop lay from his maps, but as much as he wanted to go and search, the sun was setting.

As the great orb settled below the horizon, the heat leached from the clay flats, drifting skyward and giving the demons a path up from the Core. An evil gray mist rose from the ground outside the circles, coalescing slowly into demonic form.

As the mist rose, Arlen began to feel claustrophobic, as if his circle were surrounded by glass walls, cutting him off from the world. It was hard to breathe in the circle, even though the wards blocked only demon magic, and fresh air blew across his face even now. He looked out at his rising jailors, and bared his teeth.

Wind demons were the first to form, standing about the height of a tall man at the shoulder, but with head fins that rose much higher, topping eight or nine feet. Their great long snouts were sharp-edged like beaks, but also hid rows of teeth, thick as a man's finger. Their skin was a tough, flexible armor that could turn any spearpoint or arrowhead. That resilient substance stretched thin out from their sides and along the underside of their arm bones to form the tough membrane of their giant wings, which often spanned three times their height, jointed with wicked hooked talons that could cleanly sever a man's head when they dived.

The windies took no notice of Arlen, as he was set back against the adobe walls and had yet to light his fire. As they solidified, they set off towards the riverbank at a run. Their stunted legs offered little grace on land, but as they shrieked and leapt from the edge of the bank, the cruel elegance of their design became apparent as they spread their enormous wings with a great snap and swooped upwards, flapping just a few powerful strokes before soaring into the gloaming in search of prey.

Arlen had expected to see the sand demons that haunted the dunes of the Krasian desert rise next, but the twilight showed the mists thinning already, forming only a last few wind demons.

Arlen perked up at this. Though corelings would hunt and kill most anything, their true hatred was for humanity, and they were sometimes reluctant to leave ruins once the inhabitants were dead, in case more humans were one day drawn to the site. Unaging, demons were nothing if not patient, and could lie in wait for decades or more.

It was only natural for the windies to continue to materialize here. The canyon cliffs provided an ideal takeoff spot, and they could soar far and wide in the night to seek out prey. But land-bound sand demons had no such luxury, and Arlen could find no sign of them in the area. Sand demons hunted in packs known as storms, and it seemed that some time in the last twenty years, the storm had moved on in search of other prey.

Arlen stood and began to pace impatiently as he watched the last of the wind demons go, looking up at the adobe buildings, calculating. If he kept low, it was unlikely a wind demon would spot him on the cliff walls. Even if one did, he could retreat into the adobe buildings. The windows and doorways were too narrow to admit windies unless they landed, and wind demons on land could be easily tripped or outrun. There was still no sign of sand demons;

their size and coloring would stand out in the adobe village.

And One Arm wouldn't arrive for hours. If he was quick . . .

Don't be stupid. Wait for dawn! his father's voice snapped at him, but Arlen had seldom listened to it before. If he'd wanted to live a safe life, he would have remained in the Free Cities, where most people went from womb to pyre without daring to step outside a wardnet.

Arlen had been outside in the naked night many times, especially in Fort Krasia, where he was the only outsider ever to dance *alagai'sharak*. This time, though, there were no *dal'Sharum* warriors at his side to help him if something happened. He was on his own.

Nothing new there, Arlen thought.

He lit a slow-burning fire at the center of his circle, so he might easily find his way back in the darkness, and affixed a torch socket to the end of his spear. He slung spare torches over his back in a loose pack he hoped would soon be full of Bahavan pottery. Finally, he took up his round shield, painted with the same defensive wards as his circle, and stepped over the barrier.

As he left the circle, Arlen took what felt like his first full breath since sunset. He knew it was all his imagination, but it seemed as if the air tasted better outside the circle, cooler and sweeter. It felt good to reclaim a bit of the world corelings took from man each night.

He made his way to the stairs, moving the torch this way and that, carefully scanning for any sign of demons, always ready to defend or flee.

It was a difficult climb. The steps were irregular, with some too narrow to put his entire foot upon, and others where it was several paces to the next step. Sometimes the path was nearly level, and other times it was a steep slope. He imagined the Bahavans had very strong thighs.

To make matters worse, the *dal'Sharum* had ransacked most of the lower tiers for materials to build their blockades. Broken pottery, furniture, clothing—anything not built into the walls was piled on the streets to slow any corelings on the way to Krasian ambushes that threw them over the narrow sidewall and down into the pits below.

Arlen ducked low, using the cover provided by that wall as he climbed and glanced warily out into the night sky. Wind demons could drop like silent stones from a mile in the sky, snapping their wings open at the last instant to sever a man's head, snatch him in their hind talons, and take back off without ever touching ground. He had no doubt one could pick him off the walls if it spotted him before he caught sight of it.

By the fifth tier, the blockades ended and the homes seemed intact, but Arlen continued to climb despite the burning in his thighs. Master Dravazi's workshop was said to be on the seventh tier, for there were seven pillars of heaven, and seven layers to Nie's abyss.

Arlen tried to fight back a giddy smile as he gained the seventh tier and saw the master's name carved into the archway of a large building. He scanned the area again, but there was still no sign of sand demons, and the wind demons seemed to have flown far off into the night.

A ragged curtain hung in the doorway, likely meant more to hold back the ever-present orange dust than for privacy or security. There was no need for such in a hamlet as small and isolated as Baha.

Arlen eased up to the doorway, pushing the curtain aside with the edge of his shield and thrusting his spear into the darkness. The torch cast flickering light over a room filled with pottery.

Arlen choked, hardly believing his eyes. The work lay stacked, prepared for a trip to market some twenty years ago that had never come to pass. The pottery was covered in orange dust, making it the same color as the walls and floors of the buildings, but it seemed intact, even after so much time. He reached out a tentative hand, and his fingers left lines in the dust, revealing smooth lacquer and brightly painted designs that shone in the torchlight. One room, and it contained more riches that he could possibly carry!

He dropped to one knee, setting down his spear and shield to remove the backpack. He scanned the smaller vases, lamps, and bowls, deciding what to take. He would carry a few pieces back to his circle to examine while he waited for dawn to come, and then return for the rest.

He was sliding a delicate vase into the pack when he heard the rumble. Thinking he had dislodged something and the stack of pottery was about to topple, he grabbed his spear and brought up the torch.

But there was no sign of teetering pottery, and the rumble sounded again, this time almost a growl, a few guttural "r's" floating in the darkness.

Forgetting the pottery, Arlen snatched up his shield, slowly turning towards the sound. A sand demon must have followed him into the room, stalking as quietly as it could, but unable to quell the animal instinct in its throat.

Arlen turned a slow circuit, holding his torch out far and scanning the room, but there was no sign of any demon. He gave a sudden start and glanced upwards, but there was nothing above waiting to drop on him. He shuddered and forced himself to keep looking.

He almost missed it, but for another faint growl that came while his torch happened to be in the right place. It seemed a plain adobe wall at first, but then part of the wall . . . shifted.

There was a demon there. Even staring right at it, the coreling was almost invisible. Its armor was the exact orange of the clay, and had the same rough texture. It was small, no bigger than a medium-size dog, but it was compact in a way that spoke of powerful bunched muscles, and its claws left deep grooves in the adobe walls. Arlen had never seen the like.

The coreling wriggled slightly, tamping, and then gave a great roar as it uncoiled and launched itself at him.

"Night!" Arlen screamed as he put up his shield, wondering if the wards would even hold against this new breed of coreling. Wards were picky like that, each made to block a specific type of demon. There was some overlap, but nothing to gamble one's life upon.

Magic flared as the demon struck his shield, knocking Arlen over, but even as the wards activated, Arlen knew they would not hold forever. No demon should have been able to touch his shield at all, but this one held on tenaciously against the force of the magic trying to repel it.

The demon was heavier than it looked, but Arlen got his weight under the shield and lifted, driving hard into the adobe wall. The coreling's claws lost purchase with the impact, and the magic, still pushing hard against the prone demon, flung Arlen backwards instead. He landed in the pile of pottery, smashing much of the priceless artwork.

"Corespawn it!" he cursed, but there was no time to lament, for the demon hurled itself into the pile, scattering clay shards everywhere. Arlen was jabbed and cut from all sides by the jagged clay bits as he tried to put his feet under him.

He managed to get his shield up as the clay demon leapt at him again, but the demon dug its claws in deep and pulled so hard that the leather straps around Arlen's forearm snapped, and the shield was pulled from his grasp. He stumbled frantically backwards, trying to get away from the creature before it could untangle itself and come at him again. It would be a long run back to his portable circles without his shield, and from what he had just seen, there was no guarantee his circles would even hold the creature back.

The demon leapt again, but Arlen had his spear up, stabbing the creature right in the center of its chest. It was a powerful blow from a fine weapon, but even the weakest coreling had armor enough to turn a speartip. The point failed to pierce, but the demon took the torch in its face, knocking it from its socket. Arlen shoved hard, throwing the demon back, and in the flickering light, he saw it stumble awkwardly, momentarily blinded by the light.

"Come on, then!" Arlen shouted, goading the demon as he edged towards the door. It leapt at him one last time, still dazzled, but Arlen was ready for it. Snatching the door curtain, he caught the clay demon up in its crusted and dusty folds, gripping the ends tightly as the coreling struggled. The curtain tore from the rod as Arlen pushed out the door and to the stair ledge, throwing the demon over. Still tangled in the curtain, its roars were muffled as it fell to the courtyard far below.

Arlen rushed back to snatch up the torch. He left his pack where it lay, along with his broken shield and spear, and hurried back out to the stairs. He was about to head down when a scrabbling sound vibrated in the air. He looked at the adobe walls going up the cliff face, and felt his stomach churn as they came alive with clay demons.

Gonna get'cherself killed one of these days, Arlen heard his father say, but at that moment, he had neither time nor inclination to disagree. He turned and ran down the steps as fast as his legs could carry him.

Moving faster than he could see his footing in the flickering torchlight, Arlen took steps several at a time, but it wasn't enough. There were demons ahead of him as well as behind. He must have climbed right past them on the way up, oblivious. As he came towards a landing, a pair of clay demons bounded around the corner from the tier below, talons tamping down as their muscles tensed to spring.

Arlen had no way to arrest his downward motion when they appeared, so he did the only thing he could think of and rolled right over the edge of the wall.

The drop was a good ten feet, and he landed heavily on his side on the steps of the next tier. The demons gave chase, but Arlen shoved his pain aside, bounced to his feet, and ran on.

The demons were fast, but Arlen's legs were longer, and desperation gave him blinding speed. As much from memory as from sight, he dodged around the Krasian blockades, suddenly thankful that the *dal'Sharum* had torn apart the lower levels for fodder.

A demon dropped onto him from above, talons digging deep into his back as its teeth sank into his shoulder, but Arlen hardly slowed. He shoved the torch in the demon's face and threw himself backwards into the cliff wall, blasting the breath from the creature and breaking its hold. He grabbed the coreling and threw it at another pair hurtling down the steps at him.

Using the bright torch to drive demons back, Arlen ran on. He fell twice, twisting his ankle badly once, but both times he was back up and running before the pain registered. Behind him, it seemed as if the entire cliff face had become a swarm of roaring demons.

He leapt over another wall to avoid the last infested landing and sprinted for his campfire, only to find the clay demon he had thrown over the cliff trapped in the middle of his circle. The height and cloth wrapping must have protected it from the wards on the way in, but the creature now clawed madly at the wardnet in its desperation to escape, sending spiderwebs of white magic through the air.

Unable to use his own circle, Arlen ran on to Dawn Runner's. A clay demon blocked his path, but as it leapt at him, Arlen dropped his torch and grabbed it in both hands. The demon's sharp scales cut his hands and he caught a blast of its rank breath in his face, but he pivoted sharply, using its own energy to hurl the creature into one of the demon pits in the courtyard.

There was a shriek as Arlen dove into the horse's portable circle, and the wards flared brightly as a wind demon struck the net. The coreling was hurled back and would have gone into the same pit as the clay demon had it not spread its wings in time to catch itself. It shrieked at him again, revealing rows of teeth in the light of the wards.

But Arlen wasn't safe yet. The clay demons surged at him in a wave, dozens of them charging the circle. The wards flared as the demons tried to cross the line, stopping them short, but the clay demons were not hurled back as they should be. Magic shocked through their snub bodies and they howled in pain, but still they dug their claws into the clay and inched forward against the press. Arlen moved around the circle, kicking them back from the net, but it was an impossible task to maintain for long, and it was still early in the night. Sooner or later, the clay demons would get through. Dawn Runner knew it too, the beast struggling hard against the ropes.

But then a roar sounded that dwarfed even the cacophony of the clay demons, and One Arm bounded into the courtyard. The rock demon was fifteen feet tall from horn to toe, covered in a thick black carapace that could not be harmed by anything short of the most potent wards.

Jealous as ever, the giant coreling swept the clay

demons aside with its good arm like a man might sweep autumn leaves, clearing a path to Arlen's circle. It roared at any clay demon foolish enough to draw close, killing more than a few of its smaller cousins before they took the message to heart.

Arlen had crippled One Arm in their first encounter, almost ten years gone. Little more than a boy at the time, he had severed the behemoth's limb more by accident than design, but One Arm was immortal, and as incapable of forgetting as it was of forgiveness.

Every night, One Arm rose in the place it had last seen Arlen, and followed his trail. No matter how many rivers Arlen swam or trees he climbed, the great demon always caught up to him in a matter of hours, running more swiftly than any horse. Tireless, thirstless, its only thoughts were of vengeance.

The rock demon hammered at Arlen's wards, illuminating the entire river bowl with magic as it attempted to take its revenge, but Arlen knew his rock wards well, and there was little chance that One Arm would succeed. Still, as he sat back, staring up at the enraged creature, he felt no comfort at the unexpected rescue from the clay demons. He knew that sooner or later, the mighty rock demon would catch him on the wrong side of the wards, and then he would likely wish the clay demons had gotten him.

But for now, he flung the demon an obscene gesture and dug into Dawn Runner's saddlebags for his spare herb pouch and bandages.

He had become quite good at stitching up his own skin.

Just before dawn, as the sky began to lighten, Arlen was startled awake by frantic shrieking. A light sleeper by necessity, he leapt up, shaking off slumber like a blanket. One Arm had already sunk back down into the Core, as had all the wind and clay demons save one.

The coreling trapped in Arlen's main circle smashed hard against the wardnet, clawing at the web of magic, but it was unable to pass. The wards might not be wholly attuned to clay demons, but when a coreling was surrounded on all sides by a complete circuit, the net's power was increased manifold.

The horizon brightened further, and Arlen watched the demon's last moments of existence with great interest. In the growing light, the creature looked a little like an armadillo, with segmented plates of orange armor along its back and powerful stub legs covered in thick, sharp scales and ending in hooked claws. Its blunt head was shaped like a cylinder, able to butt with tremendous force, which it demonstrated repeatedly as it smashed vainly against the magic walls of its prison.

Rays of light began to reach the dry riverbed, and the coreling screamed in pain, though the canyon walls still kept it in shadow. It wouldn't be long.

In desperation, the demon became insubstantial, disintegrating into an orange mist that filled the circle. But even its dematerialized form was unable to escape. There was no path to the Core in the clay floor inside the wardnet, and it flowed towards the edges of the circle, but crackles of magic held it at bay, shivering through the mist like lightning dancing through a cloud.

The mist flowed around the circle, trying again and again to find a hole in Arlen's tight net. Even in its disembodied state, Arlen could taste its desperation and fear, and he tensed with excitement. Demons were all but immune to mortal weapons. The only guaranteed way to kill one was to trap it in a warded circle and wait for the sun, a task that often took as many humans with it as demons.

Finally, the sun rose high enough to reach the far side of the river, and Arlen could see sparks catching in the orange cloud like kindling. Suddenly, there was a flash of intense heat as the mist ignited, setting the very air on fire. Arlen felt the rush of vacuum; his eyes dried out and his cheeks reddened, but he could not have looked away if his life depended on it. For all that demons had taken from the world, Arlen would never tire of seeing one pay the ultimate price for its evil.

He searched his campsite after the demon flame expired, but most of his gear had been torn apart and smashed by the demon, or else burned when it ignited the air. He had spares of the most irreplaceable items in Dawn Runner's circle, but that one dead demon was going to end up costing him most of his profit from selling the pottery.

If there was even pottery left to sell. Arlen rushed back up the stairs to Master Dravazi's workshop, and as he feared, almost every piece was cracked or shattered. He searched the rest of the adobe buildings and found a great deal of pottery, but it was sturdy and utilitarian. The Bahavans, dependent on trade to survive, had wasted little of their artistry on ornamenting the pieces they used themselves. He would be lucky to even cover his losses.

Still, despite the pain and loss, Arlen rode out of the canyon with his head high. He had seen someplace no one had visited in over twenty years, braved its demons, and would return to tell the tale.

One of these days, your luck won't hold, his father's voice reminded him.

Maybe, he thought back to it, *but not today*.

Abban limped through the great bazaar of Fort Krasia, the Desert Spear, leaning heavily on his crutch. He was a large-bellied man, but his lame leg would not have been able to support him in any event.

He wore a yellow silk turban topped with a tan felt cap. Under his tan suede vest he wore a loose shirt of bright blue silk, covered in thread-of-gold scrollwork, and his fingers glittered with rings. His pantaloons, the same yellow silk as his turban, were held up by a jeweled belt, and the head of his crutch was smooth white ivory, carved into the likeness of the first camel he had ever bought, with his armpit resting between its two humps.

The bazaar sprawled for miles along the inner walls of the city. There on the hot, dusty streets were seemingly endless kiosks, tents, and pens, showcasing food, spices, perfume, clothing, jewelry, furniture, livestock, pack animals, and anything else a buyer could possibly want.

Much like the Maze outside the walls, designed to let the *dal'Sharum* trap and kill any demon attempting to get into the city, the bazaar was designed to trap shoppers and put them off balance as the vendors descended on them. The dazzling array of goods and the aggressiveness of the sellers weakened the resolve and loosened the purse strings of even the most difficult-to-please shopper, and apparent exits from the district were more often than not dead ends as the ever-shifting kiosks blocked through-passage of the street. Even those familiar with the twists and turns of the bazaar found themselves lost from time to time.

But not Abban. The bazaar was his home, and the sound of shouted haggling was the air he breathed. He could no more get lost in the bazaar than the First Warrior could get lost in the Maze.

Abban was born in his family's tent, right in the center of the bazaar. His grandmother had served as midwife, and Abban's father, Chabin, had kept their kiosk open to customers even while his wife howled in the back. He couldn't afford to lose the business, especially if there was to be another mouth to feed.

Chabin was a good man, Abban remembered, a hard worker trying to provide for his family even though his cowardice had made him unsuitable as a warrior, and the clerics had found his faith lacking.

Denied those two vocations, the only callings considered suitable for a Krasian man, Abban's father had been forced to bend his back each day, toiling like a woman. He was *khaffit*, a man without honor, and the paradise of Everam would forever be denied him as a result.

But Chabin had shouldered his burdens without complaint, turning a minor kiosk of substandard trinkets into a bustling business with clients as far away as the green lands to the north. He had taught Abban about mathematics and geography, showing him how to draw words and to speak the tongue of greenlanders so that he could haggle with their Messengers over the goods they brought to trade. He taught Abban many things, but most of all, Chabin had taught Abban to fear the *dama*. A lesson provided at the cost of his own life.

Dama, the clerics of Everam, were at the highest echelon of Krasian society. They wore bright white robes that could be spotted at a distance, and served as a bridge between man and Creator. It was within the rights of the *dama* to kill any tribesman below their station, instantly and without fear of reprisal, if they felt that the man was disrespecting them or the sacred laws they enforced.

Abban had been eight when his father was killed. Cob, a Messenger from the north, had come to the kiosk, buying supplies for his return trek. He was a valued customer and a vital link to the flow of goods from the green lands. Abban knew to treat the man like a prince.

"Damaged one of my circles on the trek in," Cob said, limping with the aid of his spear. "I'll need rope and paint."

Chabin snapped his fingers, and Abban handed his father a small pot of paint while he ran to fetch the rope.

"Damned sand demon bit off half my foot before I could retreat to my spare," Cob said, showing his bandaged foot.

Distracted by the sight, neither Chabin nor Cob had noticed the *dama* passing by.

But the *dama* had noticed them; particularly that Abban's father had failed to bow low in submission, as was required of a *khaffit* in the presence of a cleric.

"Bow, you filthy *khaffit*!" the *dal'Sharum* escorting the *dama* had barked.

Chabin, startled by the shout, had whirled around,

accidentally spilling paint onto the *dama*'s pristine white robe.

For a moment, time seemed frozen, and then the enraged *dama* reached over the counter and took hold of Chabin's hair and chin, twisting sharply. A crack, like the sound of wood breaking, resounded in the tent, and Abban's father fell over, dead.

It was over a quarter century since that day, but Abban still remembered the sound vividly.

When he was old enough, Abban had been forced to try his hand at being a warrior, that he might not share his father's shame. But though Chabin's caste was not hereditary, Abban had proven just as weak, just as cowardly. He was still a novice when the brutal training crippled him, and he found himself cast out as *khaffit*.

Abban nodded at some merchants as he passed their kiosks. The vendors were mostly women, wrapped head-to-toe in heavy black cloth, though there were other *khaffit* like him, as well. They, like Abban, were easily distinguishable in their bright clothes, though all wore the plain tan cap and vest of their caste. Apart from *khaffit*, only women wore bright, colorful clothing, and they only when alone with their husbands or other women.

If the merchant women felt contempt at the sight of Abban the *khaffit*, they knew better than to show it. Though he shared his father's weaknesses, Abban had inherited Chabin's strengths as well, and the family business had grown every year since Abban had taken the reins. Offending him invariably meant a loss of business, as the fat *khaffit* had connections and ongoing deals throughout the bazaar and in cities hundreds of miles to the north. The bulk of trade from the green lands came through Abban, and any who wanted access to the valuable exotic merchandise kept their disdain to themselves.

All except one. There was a shout from across the street as Abban came to his own pavilion, and he looked with disgust at the competitor who hobbled towards him.

"Abban, my friend!" the man called, though he was anything but. "I thought I recognized your bright womanly clothes coming down the street! How is business this day?"

Abban scowled, but he knew better than to offer a rude response. Amit asu Samere am'Rajith am'Majah was a *dal'Sharum* warrior, as far above Abban the *khaffit* as a man was above a woman, and while it was not technically legal for a *dal'Sharum* to kill a *khaffit* without just cause, in practice, there would be little or no repercussion if one did.

This was why Abban had to pretend that the occasional carts of goods that vanished from his possession had never existed, much less been stolen, even when he knew it had been Amit's people who took them.

Amit was a recent addition to the market. A sand

demon had bitten the meat from his calf in battle, and the wound had festered. Eventually, the *dama'ting* had no choice but to amputate. It was a grave dishonor to be crippled in battle but not die, but since he had managed to trap the offending demon before the rising sun, Amit's place in the afterlife was assured.

Unlike Abban, Amit was clad from head to toe in black, as befitted a warrior, his night veil loose around his neck. He still carried his spear, using it more as a walking staff than a weapon these days, but he kept it sharp, and was quick to threaten with it when aroused.

A man in warrior black attracted attention in the bazaar, since it was, for the better part, the near-exclusive domain of women and *khaffit*. People tended to move carefully around him, frightened to approach, so Amit had tied a bright orange cloth beneath the head of his spear to signal his status as a merchant and to draw the eyes of potential customers.

"Ah, Amit, my good friend!" Abban said, his face filling with a look of warm, welcoming sincerity practiced before thousands of customers. "By Everam, it is good to see you. The sun shines brighter when you are about. Business is well, indeed! Thank you for asking. I trust things go well in your pavilion also?"

"Of course, of course!" Amit said, his eyes shooting daggers. He looked ready to say more, but he noticed a pair of women who had stopped to examine one of Abban's fruit carts.

"Come, come, honored mothers, I have far better

fare across the way in my pavilion!" Amit said. "Would you rather buy your goods from a soulless *khaffit*, or one who has stood tall in the night against the demon hordes?"

Few could refuse him when it was put that way, and the women turned and headed towards Amit's pavilion. Amit sneered at Abban. It was not the first time he had stolen Abban's business thusly, and likely it was not the last.

There was a hissing in the general din of the market then, and both men looked up. The sound was a warning from other vendors that *dama* approached. All around, merchants would be hiding wares that were prohibited under Evejan law, such as spirits or musical instruments. Even Amit glanced down at himself to see if he had any contraband on his person.

A few minutes later, the source of the warning became clear. Led by a young cleric in full white robe, a group of *nie'dama*, novices in white loincloths with one end thrown over their shoulders, were collecting bread, fruit, and meat from the market. There was no offer of payment for what they took, nor did any vendor dare ask. The *dama* grazed like goats, and there was nothing a merchant who valued his skin dare say about it.

Remembering his father's lesson, Abban bowed so low when the *dama* appeared that he feared he might tip over. Amit noticed, and smacked Abban's crutch with the butt of his spear, braying a laugh as Abban fell in the dust. The *dama* turned their way at the sound, and Abban, feeling the weight of that look, put his forehead down and groveled in the dirt like a dog. Amit, conversely, simply nodded his head to the *dama* in respect, a gesture the cleric returned.

The *dama* walked on after a moment, but Abban caught the eye of one of the *nie'dama*, a skinny boy of no more than twelve years. The boy glanced at Amit, then smirked at Abban kneeling in the dust, but he winked conspiratorially before following after his brothers.

And to make matters worse, that was the precise moment the Par'chin arrived.

Being caught groveling in the dirt was never a good way to begin a negotiation.

Arlen looked sadly at Abban kneeling in the dirt. He knew the loss of face hurt his friend more deeply than a *dama*'s whip ever could. There were a great many things that Arlen admired about the Krasian people, but their treatment of women and *khaffit* was not among them. No man deserved such shame.

He looked away purposefully as Abban hauled on his crutch to regain his feet, staring intently at a cart of trinkets he had no interest in. When Abban had righted himself and dusted off, Arlen led Dawn Runner over as if he had just arrived.

"Par'chin!" Abban cried, as if he had just noticed

Arlen himself. "It is good to see you, son of Jeph! I take it from the laden horse you lead that your journey was a success?"

Arlen pulled out a Dravazi vase, handing it to Abban for inspection. As ever, Abban had a look of disgust painted on his face before he even had a good look at the object. He reminded Arlen of old Hog, the owner of the general store in Tibbet's Brook where he had grown up. Never one to let a seller know he was interested until the haggling was done.

"Pity, I had hoped for better," Abban said, though the vase was more beautiful than any Arlen had ever seen in Abban's pavilion. "I doubt it will sell for much."

"Spare me the demonshit, for once," Arlen snapped. "I almost got myself cored over these pieces, and if you're not paying good coin for them, I'll take them elsewhere."

"You wound me, son of Jeph!" Abban cried. "I, who gave you the very maps and instruction that led you to the treasure in the first place!"

"The place was full of strange demons," Arlen said. "That drives the price up."

"Strange demons?" Abban asked.

Arlen nodded. "They were snub and orange like the rock," he said, "no bigger than a dog, but there were hundreds of them."

Abban nodded. "Clay demons," he said. "Baha kad'Everam is infested with them."

"Night, you knew?!" Arlen cried. "You knew and sent me there unprepared?"

"I didn't tell you about the clay demons?" Abban asked.

"No, you corespawned well didn't!" Arlen shouted. "I didn't even have proper wards against them!"

Abban paled. "What do you mean, you didn't have wards against them, Par'chin?" he said. "Any fool child knows about clay demons."

"If you were born in a ripping desert, maybe!" Arlen growled. "They told me the same thing in the corespawned Duke's Mines after I was almost cored by a snow demon. I should take this whole load north to Fort Rizon, just to spite you!"

"Oh, there's no need for that, Par'chin!" a voice called. Arlen looked up to see a *dal'Sharum* hobbling across the street to them. He didn't know the man, but it was no surprise the man knew him. Most *dal'Sharum* had at least heard of the Par'chin, if not met him directly.

By itself, *chin* meant "outsider," but in practice it was an insult, synonymous with "coward" and "weakling." It was a title even lower than *khaffit*. "Par'chin," however, meant "brave outsider," and it was a singular title belonging to Arlen alone, the only greenlander ever to learn the ways of the Desert Spear and stand beside *dal'Sharum* in *alagai'sharak*.

"Allow me to introduce myself," the stranger said in Krasian, gripping forearms with Arlen in a warrior's greeting. He didn't speak the northern tongue as Abban did, but unlike most other Messengers, Arlen spoke the Krasian tongue fluently. "I am Amit asu Samere am'Rajith am'Majah," the man said. "Tell me how this pathetic *khaffit* has failed you, and I will better anything he has offered."

Abban grabbed Arlen's arm. "Tell him you stole pottery from hallowed ground, Par'chin," he said in the Northern tongue, "and we'll both be staked out before the city gates as night falls."

"*Khaffit!*" Amit barked. "It is the height of rudeness to speak some barbarian tongue in the presence of men!"

"A thousand apologies, noble *dal'Sharum*," Abban said, bowing low and stepping back so the other man could not trip him again.

"You don't want to deal with the likes of this pig-eating half-man," Amit said to Arlen. "You have stood in the night! Dealing with *khaffit* is beneath you. But like you, I have demon ichor on my hands. Twelve, did I help see the sun, before losing my leg!"

"Ah," Abban muttered in Arlen's language, "the last time I heard him tell it, it was only a half dozen. He must be adding to his count still."

"Eh, what was that, *khaffit*?" Amit asked, not understanding, but knowing it was likely an insult.

"Nothing, honored *dal'Sharum*," Abban said, bowing smugly.

Amit smacked Abban's face. "I told you before you

were being rude with that savage grunting!" he barked. "Apologize to the Par'chin!"

Arlen had had enough. He stamped his spear, rounding on the merchant angrily. "You would ask a man to apologize for speaking my own language to me?!" he roared, shoving Amit so hard he fell to the ground. For a moment, the merchant's eyes hardened and he gripped his spear, ready to leap to the attack, but his eyes flicked to Arlen's strong legs, and then to his own stump, and he thought better of it. He bowed his head.

"My apologies, Par'chin." He bit off the words as if each one had a foul taste. "I meant no insult."

The caste system cut both ways. Amit had greeted Arlen as a fellow warrior, and warriors had their own pecking order: strong to weak. His peg leg put Amit at the very bottom of that order. To a strong warrior, he was only a small step above *khaffit* himself. It was no wonder Amit had chosen to make the bazaar his home.

Arlen pointed his spear at Amit. "Think twice before you insult my homeland again," he said, keeping his voice low with menace, "or the next time the dust of the street will be dampened with blood."

He meant no such thing, of course, but Amit need never know that. *Dal'Sharum* required a show of strength, if they were to respect you.

Abban took Arlen's arm and hurried him into his pavilion before the incident had a chance to escalate further.

"Hah!" he cried, when they were inside and the heavy tent flap closed behind them. "Amit will make me suffer a month for seeing that, but it will be worth every insult and blow."

"You shouldn't have to tolerate such treatment," Arlen said for what felt like the thousandth time. "It's not right."

But Abban waved him away. "Right or wrong, it is the way of things, Par'chin," Abban said. "Perhaps they treat my kind differently in your land, but in the Desert Spear, you might as well ask the sun not to shine so hot."

It was cool in Abban's tent, and his women came over immediately, taking Arlen's dusty outer robe and his boots, giving him a clean robe to sit in. They piled pillows for the men and brought out pitchers of water and bowls of fruit and meat, along with steaming cups of tea. When they were refreshed, Abban produced a small bottle and two tiny clay cups.

"Come, Par'chin, drink with me," he said. "Let us calm our nerves and start our meeting anew." Arlen looked at the tiny cup dubiously, then shrugged and took a sip.

A moment later, he spit it back out, reaching frantically for the water jug. Abban laughed and kicked his feet.

"Are you trying to poison me?" Arlen demanded, but his anger dissipated when Abban held up his own cup and drained it.

"What in the Core is that foul brew?" he asked.

"Couzi," Abban said. "Made from distilled fermented grain and cinnamon. By Everam, Par'chin, how many casks of it have you lugged across the desert without having a taste?"

"I don't drink the merchandise," Arlen said. "And for the ledger, it tastes more like a flame demon's spit than cinnamon."

"It can double as lamp oil," Abban agreed, smiling. He refilled Arlen's cup and handed it to him. "Best to drink the first one quickly," he advised, refilling his own cup, "but by the third, all you'll taste is the cinnamon."

Arlen threw back the cup and nearly choked. His throat burned like he had just drunk boiling water.

"This is a corespawned drink," he choked, but he allowed Abban to fill his cup again.

"The Damaji agree with you, Par'chin," Abban said. "Couzi is illegal under Evejan law, but we *khaffit* are allowed to make it to sell to *chin*."

"And you keep a little for yourself," Arlen said.

Abban snorted. "I do more business in couzi here than in the green lands, Par'chin," he said. "It takes only a small bottle to make even a large man's head swim, so it is easily smuggled under the *dama*'s noses. *Khaffit* drink it by the cask, and *dal'Sharum* bring it into the Maze to give them bravery in the night. Even a few *dama* have developed the taste."

"You don't think it'll cost you in the next life, selling

forbidden drink to clerics?" Arlen asked, draining another cup. Already, it was going down smoother.

"If I believed in such nonsense, I would, Par'chin," Abban said, "so it is well that I don't."

Arlen sipped at the next cup, his throat numb to the burn now. He savored the taste of the cinnamon, amazed that he hadn't noticed it before. He felt as if his body were floating above the embroidered silk pillows he rested upon. Abban seemed similarly relaxed, and by the time the small bottle was empty, they were laughing at nothing and slapping one another on the back.

"Now that we're friends again," Abban said, "may we return to business?"

Arlen nodded, and watched as Abban rose unsteadily to his feet, stumbling over to the Bahavan pottery that his women had unloaded from Dawn Runner and brought inside. Of course, Abban's face immediately fell into one of practiced neutrality as he prepared to haggle.

"Most of these are not Dravazi," he said.

"Wasn't much in the master's shop," Arlen lied. "Besides, we still need to discuss your lack of candor regarding the dangers of the trip before we talk coin."

"What does it matter?" Abban asked. "You walked out unscathed, as always."

"It matters, because I might not have gone at all if I had known the place was infested with demons I didn't have proper wards for!" Arlen snapped.

But Abban only scoffed, waving a hand at him dismissively. "What reason would I have had to lie to you, son of Jeph?" he asked. "You are the Par'chin, the brave one who dares to go anywhere! Had I told you of the clay demons, it would only have strengthened your resolve to see the place and spit in their eyes!"

"Flattery ent gonna get you out of this, Abban," Arlen said, though the compliment did warm his couzied mind a bit. "You'll need to do better."

"What would the Par'chin have me do?" Abban asked.

"I want a grimoire of clay demon wards," Arlen said.

"Done," Abban said, "and free of charge. My gift to you, my friend." Arlen raised his eyebrows. Wards were a valuable commodity, and Abban was not a man free with his gifts.

"Call it investment," Abban said. "Even plain Baha-van pottery has value. A little hint of danger to make a buyer feel he's getting something rare." He looked at Arlen. "There's more in the village?" he asked.

Arlen nodded.

"Well," Abban said, "there's no profit in you getting killed before you can haul it back."

"Fair enough," Arlen said. "But still, how can you just offer something like that? Aren't books of warding forbidden for you to even touch?"

Abban chuckled. "Most everything is forbidden to a *khaffit*, Par'chin. But yes, the *dama* consider warding a holy task and guard the art closely."

"But you can get me a grimoire of clay demon wards," Arlen said.

"Right out from under the *dama*'s noses!" Abban laughed, snapping his fingers under Arlen's nose. Arlen stumbled drunkenly, falling back onto the pile of pillows, and both of them laughed again.

"How?" Arlen pressed.

"Ah, my friend," Abban waved an admonishing finger at Arlen, "you ask me to give away too much of my trade secret."

"Demonshit," Arlen said. "Your map to Baha was off by more than a day. If I'm to trust my life to these maps and wards you give me, I want to know the information is good."

Abban looked at him for a long moment, then shrugged and sat back down beside Arlen. He snapped his fingers, and one of his black-clad women brought another bottle of couzi. She knelt to fill their cups before bowing low and leaving them. They clicked cups and drank.

Abban leaned in close. "I will tell you this, Par'chin," he said quietly, "not because you are a valued client, but because you are my true friend. The Par'chin has never treated this lowly *khaffit* as anything but a man."

Arlen scoffed, refilling their cups. "You *are* a man," he said.

Abban bowed his head in gratitude and leaned in close again. "It is my nephew, Jamere," he confided.

"His father was *dal'Sharum*, but died while the boy was still in swaddling. The father's family had little wealth, so my sister returned to my pavilion, and raised the boy here in the bazaar. He recently came of age and was taken to find his life's path, but he is scrawny, and the *dal'Sharum* drillmasters were unimpressed with him. His wit, however, impressed the *dama*, and he was taken as an acolyte."

"He was one of the *nie'dama* in the market today?" Arlen asked, and Abban nodded.

"Jamere may be a cleric in training," Abban said, "but the boy is utterly corrupt, and has even less faith than I do. He will happily copy or steal any scroll in the temple if I tell him there's a buyer and share the profits."

"Any scroll?" Arlen asked.

"Anything!" Abban bragged, snapping his fingers again. "Why, he could steal even the maps to the lost city of Anoch Sun!"

Arlen felt his heart stop. Anoch Sun was the ancient seat of power of Kaji, the man the Krasians worshipped as the first Deliverer. Three thousand years earlier, give or take a few centuries, Kaji had conquered the known world—the desert and the green lands beyond—and united all mankind in war against the corelings. Using magical warded weapons, they slaughtered demons in such great numbers that for centuries it was believed that they had won, the corelings were extinct, and the night was free.

But it was a fleeting victory in the great scheme, as everyone now knew. The demons had retreated to the Core, where none could follow, and they had waited. Waited for their enemies to grow old and die. And their children. And their children's children. Immortal, the corelings had waited until the surface of the world had all but forgotten their existence. Until demons were nothing more than myth, and the ancient symbols of power that man had used against them were forgotten bits of folklore.

They had waited. And bred. And when they returned, they took back all they had lost and more.

The basic wards of forbiddance and protection had been found in time to save a few pockets of humanity, but the ancient combat wards of Kaji, wards that could make a mortal weapon powerful enough to bite into demonic flesh, were lost. Arlen had spent years searching ruins for a sign of them, but had yet to find a hint of evidence that they had even truly existed, much less the wards themselves.

But if they were anywhere, they were in Anoch Sun. When the Krasians prayed, they knelt to the northwest, where the city was supposed to lay. Arlen had looked for the lost city twice before, but there were thousands of square miles of desert in that direction, and his searches had felt like looking for a particular grain in a sandstorm.

"You get me a map to Anoch Sun," Arlen said, "and you can have the lot of Bahavan pottery for nothing.

I'll even go back with a cart for another load, on my own coin."

Abban's eyes widened in shock, then he brayed a laugh and shook his head. "Surely you know I was joking, Par'chin," he said. "The lost city of Kaji is a myth."

"It isn't," Arlen said. "I read of it in the histories in the Duke's Library in Fort Miln. The city exists, or did, once."

Abban's eyes narrowed. "Let us say you are correct, and I could procure this," he said. "The Holy City is sacred. If the *dama* ever learned you went there, both our lives would be forfeit."

"How is that different from Baha kad'Everam?" Arlen asked. "Didn't you say looting the ruins for pottery would mark us both a death sentence if we were caught?"

"It is as different as night and day, Par'chin," Abban said. "Baha is nothing, a camelpiss hamlet full of *khaffit*. The *dal'Sharum* danced *alagai'sharak* there to hallow the graves of the Bahavans only out of obligation to Evejan law, to allow its inhabitants a chance to be reincarnated into a higher caste. Besides, there is Dravazi pottery in every palace in Krasia. The only notice a few new pieces added to the market will draw will be from eager buyers.

"Anoch Sun, on the other hump, is the holiest place in the world," Abban said. "If you, a *chin*, were to desecrate it, every man, woman, and child in Krasia would cry for your head. And any artifacts you returned with would draw many questions."

"I would never desecrate anything!" Arlen said. "I've studied the ancient world my entire life. I would treat the find with more reverence than anyone."

"Simply setting foot there would be a desecration, Par'chin," Abban said.

"Demonshit," Arlen snapped. "No one has been there in thousands of years, a time when Kaji's empire extended over my people's lands as well as yours. I have as much right to go there as anyone."

"That may be, Par'chin," Abban said, "but you will find few in Krasia who will agree with you."

"I don't care," Arlen said, looking Abban hard in the eyes. "Either you get me that map, or I take the Dravazi pottery north and start selling my northern contacts' goods to other vendors in the bazaar."

Abban stared back at him for some time, and Arlen could practically hear the abacus beads clicking in his friend's head as he calculated the loss of Arlen's business. There were few Messengers willing to brave the dangers of the Krasian Desert and its people. Arlen came to the Desert Spear three times as often as other Messengers, and he spoke the Krasian tongue well enough to take his business elsewhere.

"Very well, Par'chin," Abban said at last, "but be it upon your head, if it comes back upon you. I will deal in no Sunian artifacts."

That surprised Arlen, who knew Abban was not one to turn down any chance at profit.

A fool's a man who knows better and does the thing anyway, his father's voice said.

Arlen pushed the thought aside. The call of the lost city was too great, and worth any risk.

"I'll never breathe a word of it," he promised.

"I will get a message to my nephew this evening," Abban said. "There is a lesser *dama* who comes to me for couzi each night, and he carries messages to the boy in exchange. He will reply tomorrow telling us how long the texts we require will take to copy, and where and when to meet him to make the exchange. You'll have to come with me to that, Par'chin. I won't smuggle a map to Anoch Sun through my tent."

Arlen nodded. "Anything you need, my friend," he said.

"I hope you mean that, Par'chin," Abban said.

"We'll need to wear these," Abban said, holding up black *dal'Sharum* robes. Arlen stared at him in surprise. Even though he sometimes fought beside *dal'Sharum* in the Maze, Arlen was not allowed to wear the black, and Abban . . .

"What will happen if we're caught wearing those?" he asked.

Abban took a swig of couzi right from the bottle and passed it to Arlen. "Best not dwell on such things," he said. "We'll be doing the exchange at night, and the robes should hide us well in the darkness. Even if we are seen, the night veils will add a measure of disguise, so long as we outrun any who see us."

Arlen looked at Abban's lame leg doubtfully, but made no mention of it. "We're going out at night?" he asked. "Isn't that forbidden under Evejan law?"

"What about this Nie-spawned transaction isn't, Par'chin?" Abban snapped, grabbing the couzi bottle and drinking again. "The city is well warded. There hasn't been a demon on the streets of Krasia in living memory."

Arlen shrugged. "Makes no difference to me," he said.

"Of course not," Abban muttered, taking another pull of couzi. "The Par'chin fears nothing."

They waited for the sun to set, and then slipped into the black warrior robes. Arlen admired himself in one of Abban's many mirrors, surprised to see that with a bit of makeup around his eyes and his night veil drawn, he looked just like any other Krasian warrior, if a few inches shorter.

Abban, on the other hand, would not withstand close scrutiny. He was tall like a warrior, but without his crutch, he leaned heavily on his spear, and the bulk stretching the robes about his midsection was most unlike a warrior's lean form.

It was full dark when they opened the tent flap and looked outside. In the distance, Arlen heard the signal horns of the *dal'Sharum* and the reports of their artillery, and longed to fight beside them.

Anything is safer than that, the voice in his head said, and for once, Arlen agreed. *Alagai'sharak* was a beautiful madness, but without the combat wards of old, it was madness nonetheless. But the way of the north, cowering behind wards each night, was no saner. One way killed the men's bodies, and the other, their spirits. The world needed a third choice, but only the wards of old could give it to them.

They rode a small camel cart to their destination. The camel's feet, as well as the wheels of the cart, were wrapped in cushioned leather for silence, and whispered in the dusty sandstone streets. They dared no light as they crossed the city, but the stars in the desert were bright, and the flashing of the wards in the Maze was like lightning, illuminating everything for a moment at random intervals.

"We meet Jamere at Sharik Hora, the temple of Heroes' Bones," Abban said. "He cannot venture far from the acolyte cells."

Arlen weathered a moment's guilt. Mammoth Sharik Hora was both temple and graveyard, the entire structure built from the *dal'Sharum* who had died in *alagai'sharak*. The mortar was mixed with their blood. Their bones and skin composed the furniture. Hundreds of thousands, perhaps millions of warriors had given their lives for its ideals and their bodies for its walls and domed ceiling.

There was no holier place in Fort Krasia than Sharik Hora, and here he was, sneaking in the night to steal from its walls. Like Baha kad'Everam. Like Anoch Sun.

Is that all I am? Arlen wondered to himself. *A grave robber? A man without honor?*

He almost asked Abban to turn back. But then, he thought of the huge temple, and how the *dal'Sharum* could not even fill the seats anymore, because of their endless war of attrition. All because a group of Holy Men hoarded knowledge. The Tenders of the northland were much the same, and Arlen had never hesitated to ignore their rules.

They're only copies, he told himself. *Ent stealing, just forcing them to share.*

It still ent right, his father said in his head.

They left the cart in an alley two blocks away, and went the rest of the way on foot. The streets were utterly deserted. As they approached the temple, Abban tied a bright cloth to the end of his spear, waving it back and forth. After a moment, a similar cloth was waved from a window on the second story.

"That way, quickly," Abban said, hobbling towards the window as fast as his lame leg would allow. "If they catch Jamere out of his cell . . ." He left the thought unfinished, but Arlen could easily imagine the rest.

As they put their backs to the temple wall, a thin silk rope was slung down from the window. The boy who slid down it may have been skinny, but he moved with the fluid grace of a warrior. The *dama* were masters of the brutal Krasian art of weaponless combat known as *sharusahk*. Arlen had studied the art with its greatest teachers amongst the *dal'Sharum*, but while it was only part of a warrior's overall training, the *dama* devoted their lives to the practice. Arlen had never seen one of them actually fight—no one was fool enough to attack a *dama*—but he saw how they moved, always in perfect balance and awareness. He did not doubt that they were masters of killing men.

"I've only a moment, Uncle," the boy said, pressing a leather satchel into Abban's hands. "I think someone heard me. I need to get back before I am seen, or they perform a bido count."

Abban produced a pouch that clinked heavily with coin, but the boy held up his hand. "Later," he said. "I don't want it with me if I'm caught."

"Nie's black heart," Abban muttered. "Get ready to run," he told Arlen, handing him the satchel.

"I'll give the money to your mother," Abban told Jamere.

"Don't you dare!" the boy hissed. "The witch will steal it. I'll come for it later, and you had best have it ready!"

He went and gripped his rope, but before he could begin to climb, a flickering light blossomed in the window above, and there was a shout as the rope was spotted.

"Run!" Abban whispered harshly, using the spear

to hop along at an impressive pace. Arlen followed, and when a white robed *dama* stuck a lamp out the window and spotted them, the boy came hurrying after, muttering Krasian curses too fast for Arlen to follow.

"You there! Stop!" the cleric cried. Lights began to blossom in the temple windows, and the *dama* leapt from the window, disregarding the rope entirely. He hit the sandstone street in a roll, heading right for them even as he exhausted the fall's momentum. He was back on his feet in a moment, sprinting hard after them.

"Stop and face Everam's justice!" he screamed.

But all three of them knew that "Everam's justice" meant only a quick death, and wisely ran on, turning a corner and breaking the cleric's line of sight momentarily.

Abban was slowing them, huffing as he hobbled on his spear. He stumbled suddenly, falling to his knees and dropping his spear. He looked at Arlen with frantic eyes.

"Do not leave me!" he begged.

"Don't be an idiot," Arlen snapped, grabbing his arm and hauling the fat merchant upright.

"Get Abban to the cart," Arlen told Jamere. "I will delay the *dama*."

"No, I'll do it," Jamere said. "I can . . ."

"Mind your elders, boy," Arlen said, shocked to hear one of his father's phrases pass his own lips. He grabbed the boy's arm and propelled him towards Abban. The boy looked at him as if he were mad, but Arlen glared at him and he nodded and tucked himself under Abban's arm.

Arlen slipped into a shadow, his black robes making him invisible in the night, and slung the satchel over his shoulders. If anyone was caught with the evidence, let it be him.

Right fix you've gotten yourself into now, the voice in his head observed.

The *dama* came around the corner at a run, but still he was ready for Arlen's ambush, ducking smoothly beneath a circle kick that would have blown across his solar plexus. The *dama* rolled by, then straightened suddenly, his stiffened fingers striking Arlen in the wrist.

Arlen's hand went numb, and his spear fell away from his nerveless fingers as the *dama* dropped low and spun to sweep his legs. Arlen threw himself backwards, tumbling until he could spring back to his feet. The *dama* came at him hard, a white-robed specter of death.

They met on even footing and traded furious blows. For the first few moments, Arlen thought he might have a chance, but it quickly became clear the *dama* was only taking his measure. He twisted sharply away from one of Arlen's kicks, pivoting back to punch Arlen hard in the throat.

It was not like having the wind knocked out of him,

which Arlen had experienced many times. This was like having the wind trapped within him, its means of egress and replenishment cut off. He choked, staggering, and the *dama* turned almost lazily into the kick to his stomach that forced the breath back out of his damaged windpipe with a blast of agony and sent him flying onto his back in the street.

Arlen could hear other *dama* approaching from Sharik Hora, and see the flicker of their lamps. He struggled to rise as the *dama* coldly advanced upon him.

"Who were your accomplices, servant of Nie?" the *dama* asked. "Tell me the names of the lame one and the boy, and I will grant you a quick death."

Arlen tensed to attack again, and the *dama* laughed. "Your *sharusahk* is pitiful, fool. You only prolong your pain."

Arlen knew the man was right, he was the superior fighter. But combat was more than perfection of art. Combat was doing whatever was required to win.

He grabbed a fistful of sand from the street and flung it into the *dama*'s eyes, kicking hard at his knee even as the cleric cried out and clutched his face. There was a satisfying crack, and the *dama* dropped screaming to the ground.

Arlen staggered to his feet, running after Abban and the boy. They were on the cart now, and Arlen leapt aboard just as Abban whipped the camel and the beast galloped away.

Behind them, half a dozen clerics gave chase, all carrying lanterns and moving with the same impossible grace and speed.

Abban whipped the poor camel raw, and slowly they began to pull away, as the beast reached speeds no man could match. Arlen dared to think they might escape when they hit a pit in the road and one of the cart's two wheels shattered. All three were thrown to the ground, and the camel stopped, the heavy beast laboring for breath.

"To the abyss with you both," Jamere said. "I'm not dying for a *chin* and a *khaffit*." He leapt to his feet and ran towards the *dama*.

"Mercy, masters!" the boy cried, falling to his knees before them. "I was but a hostage!"

Arlen didn't stop to stare. "Get on!" he shouted, shoving Abban at the camel as he produced a wicked knife to slice the leather harnesses that held the beast to the broken cart. The moment it was free, he stuck one foot in the stirrup, grabbed the saddle horn, and slapped the camel hard on the rump with the flat of his blade. The beast gave a great bray and broke into a run, leaving the cries of the *dama* behind.

"Take the books and go at first light, Par'chin," Abban said. "Leave the city, and I will bribe the gate guards to swear you've been gone for a week."

"What about you?" Arlen asked.

"I will be better off with you and the evidence long gone," Abban said. "Jamere will tell them he could not see our identities with the night veils in place, and without proof, a few well-placed bribes will divert any inquiry."

Arlen nodded, and bowed. "Thank you, my friend," he said. "I'm sorry to have caused you so much trouble."

Abban clapped his shoulder. "I am sorry, too, Par'chin. I should have better warned you about the dangers of Baha kad'Everam. Let us call the account settled." They shook hands, and Arlen headed out into the night.

At dawn, he returned to his hostel, pretending to be returning from *alagai'sharak*. No one questioned this, and he was able to retrieve his possessions and escape Fort Krasia before most of its inhabitants left the undercity. The *dal'Sharum* at the gates even lifted their spears to him as he left.

As he rode, he clutched the precious map tube. He would go to Fort Rizon and resupply, and then he would find Anoch Sun.

There was a hissing in the bazaar, as the merchants warned of approaching *dama*.

Abban hurriedly drew back into his tent, peeking through the narrow gap in the flaps as a group of black-clad *dal'Sharum* warriors appeared, shoving people aside as they escorted a group of furious looking *dama* and a young, skinny acolyte. Abban's fingers tightened on the canvas as they marched up the street, stopping in front of his pavilion.

Amit came limping up to them, the crippled *dal'Sharum* bowing his head slightly. "Have you come for the *khaffit*, finally?" he asked one of the warriors. "Whatever you think he has done, I assure you it is the least of his crimes . . ."

He was cut off, as the *dal'Sharum* struck him across the face with the butt of his spear. Blood and teeth exploded from the merchant's mouth as he fell to the dust. He tried to rise, but the warrior that had struck him leapt around behind him, putting his spear under Amit's chin and his knee into his back, pulling hard to choke Amit's head upwards to look at the *dama* and boy.

"Is this the one?" the lead *dama* asked the boy.

"Yes," Jamere said. "He said he would kill my mother, if I did not obey."

"What?!" Amit gasped. "I've never seen you before in my. . . !" Again the warrior pulled back on the spear, and his words were cut off with a gurgle.

"Do you recognize this?" the *dama* asked, holding up the spear Abban had dropped in the street, tied with the bright orange cloth he had used to signal Jamere. "Do you think us stupid? It's no secret you wear a womanly orange kerchief on your vestigial weapon, cripple."

"*Dama*, see here," a warrior cried, leading a camel

from Amit's pen. "It's been whipped recently, and wears leather pads on its feet."

Amit's eyes bulged, though it was hard to tell if it was from incredulity or the continually choking spear at his throat. "That's not my. . . !" was all he managed to cough.

"Tell us who your accomplice was," the *dama* demanded. The warrior at Amit's back eased the choking spear so he could answer.

Gone was all the smug superiority from Amit's voice, the security in his position in this world and the next. Abban listened carefully, savoring the pathetic desperation in his rival's voice as he protested his innocence and begged for his life.

"Tear the black from him," the *dama* ordered, and Amit screamed as the warriors took hold of his robes, ripping at them until the crippled man was lying naked in the street. The *dal'Sharum* took his arms and pulled back on his hair to ensure he made eye contact with the *dama*, who knelt before him.

"You are *khaffit* now, Amit of no lineage worth mentioning," the *dama* said. "For the short, painful remainder of your life, know this, for when your spirit leaves this world, it will forever sit outside the gates of Heaven."

"Nooo!" Amit screamed. "It is a lie!"

The *dama* looked up at the warriors. "Confiscate everything of value in his pavilion," he said, "and bring it to the temple. Use his women, if you like,

and then have them sold. Put any sons to the spear."
Amit howled, thrashing against the men who held
his arms until one of the warriors clubbed him in
the back of the head with his spear, dropping him
senseless to the ground.

The *dama* looked down at Amit in disgust. "Haul
this filth to the Chamber of Eternal Sorrow," he told
the *dal'Sharum*, "that the Damaji might take their
time in flaying the skin from his misbegotten bones."

Abban let the tent flap fall and retreated into his
pavilion, pouring himself a cup of couzi.

A few moments later, the tent flap rose and fell
again.

"The Par'chin nearly broke Dama Kavere's knee,"
Jamere said. "He wants more than couzi to account
for it."

Abban nodded, expecting as much. "You were supposed to volunteer to stall Kavere when I stumbled,
not the Par'chin," Abban reminded.

Jamere shrugged. "He beat me to it," he said, "and
would hear no protest."

"Well don't let it happen again," Abban snapped.
"The Par'chin is valuable to me, and I would be most
displeased to lose him."

"Do you think he'll find Anoch Sun?" Jamere asked.

Abban laughed. "Don't be stupid, boy," he said.
"Those maps have been copied and recopied for
three thousand years, and even if they still manage to
point him the right way, the lost city, if it even exists, is

buried deep beneath the sands. The Par'chin is a good-hearted fool, but a fool nonetheless."

"He'll be angry, when he returns," Jamere observed.

Abban shrugged. "At first, perhaps," he began.

"But then you'll wave some other ancient scroll in his face, and he'll forget all about it," Jamere guessed, stealing a swig out of Abban's couzi bottle, not bothering with a cup.

Abban smiled, giving the boy the various bribes he would need when he returned to Sharik Hora. He watched Jamere go with a mix of pride and profound regret.

The boy could really have been something, if he wasn't set to waste his life as a *dama*.

DELETED SCENES

There were a great many deleted scenes from *The Warded Man*. Some were cut for length (I had written an extremely long book by debut novel standards), or for pacing, or because they went off on tangents and reduced overall tension.

However, many of those deleted scenes are nice little stories in their own right, and it's wonderful that Tachyon has given me the opportunity to share a couple of them, along with my commentary, in this great collection. What's best about the selections presented is that they are self-contained story arcs, and can be enjoyed by new readers and fans of the series alike.

ARLEN

Introduction

This scene is how it all started. I was taking a fantasy writing class in 1999, and we were given a homework assignment to "write the first scene of an original fantasy novel." I wrote a little story about a young boy named Arlen who was never allowed to go farther from home than he could get by midday, because he needed to get back home before the demons came out at night.

To be honest, I knocked the story out in one night, and after I got my grade (an A, natch), I threw it in a drawer for years. At the time, I was working on a different book, but Arlen was never far from my thoughts, and every once in a while I would jot down a few notes on his world. The entire *Warded Man* series grew out of this 1600 word story.

Why It Was Cut

This opening was one of the biggest points of contention between me and my editor. She felt quite strongly that prologues in general were obsolete, and that this one was also told in a very different voice than the rest of the book and didn't fit. She also thought it didn't add anything that couldn't be shown elsewhere. I couldn't have disagreed more, believing that it set the mood and scene perfectly, and was a view into young Arlen's personality that was essential.

We had some . . . lively debates on the subject. I have a great deal of respect for my editor, and I tried very hard to see her side of things. It took me a while to separate my personal attachment to the scene to the point where I could consider things impartially. When I finally managed to do so, I realized that she was right, and cut the scene. I think the book as a whole works better without it, though on a personal level, it is still very near and dear to my heart. It makes me really happy to see it in print at last.

When Arlen was a boy, he would play outside until the last moment of dusk before answering his mother's calls. There was nothing worse than being locked inside each night, and he was determined not to let a minute of daylight be wasted indoors.

He would rise while darkness still reigned, stepping over the threshold of his family farmhouse before even the cock could crow, just as the first beams of sunlight topped the hills, brightening the reddened sky and sending the shadows scurrying away for another day. His mother wanted him to count to a hundred after that, but he never listened.

Adventure awaited, but Arlen knew his chores came first. Snatching the cloth-lined wicker basket from where it lay by the door, he would run to the chicken coop, ignoring the squawks of protest as he gathered the eggs, handling them as deftly as the colored balls of a Jongleur.

With a dash back to the house, he left the eggs for his mother to find and was outside again in a moment. Before his father could pull on his overalls, before his mother had changed from her nightdress, Arlen was on a stool beneath the first of the cows. He left the milk and rushed to the rest of his chores while his father ate breakfast. The well house, the curing shed, the smokehouse, the silo, each was paid a hurried visit, as if he were but a breeze passing through the farm.

There was something comforting about the morning ritual. It reaffirmed his bond with the land, a bond severed each night as his mother locked the doors and his father checked the wards on the windows.

He let the animals out of the barn, guiding the

pigs to their day-pen and the sheep to the pasture with cracks of a switch. He fed the swine and the horse, paying the sheep little mind. Even without the dogs to mind them, they would not venture past the wardposts, for the grass beyond was scorched and ruined.

There were other chores, less frequent, less comforting. Once in a while it happened that some animal or another was not where it was supposed to be by dusk, and was lost. He would find it the next morning, torn to shreds, and bury it behind the outhouse.

Arlen had done it all a thousand times, and he went about his duties with such practiced efficiency that by midmorning, he was usually done. By then, his father was well out into the fields checking the wardposts, and so he went back to the house for the familiar breakfast: oats, eggs, and bacon kept warm by his mother. He'd wolf it all down without a pause for air. A gulp of milk to help him swallow, and he was bouncing from his seat.

His mother caught him. She always did. There was always something for him to do in the house, the chores he hated most. But there was no denying his mother, and complaining would not fill the firebox, or sweep the floor, or put fresh charcoal sticks in the warding kit. "Yarn doesn't make itself," she would tell him.

By midday, he was free. Before his father returned from the fields with new chores for him, Arlen would snatch some bread and cheese and dash off to eat his lunch. Like his breakfast, he hardly tasted it. Food was sustenance, nothing more.

How far can I get today? he would ask himself as he ate his lunch. With nearly eight hours until dusk, he could head off in any direction he wanted for four. The sun's place in the sky would tell him when to turn back.

It was a dangerous game, one the other children of Tibbet's Brook dared not play. It was one of a thousand ways Arlen differed from them. All of the others were content to live in the Brook, never caring what lay over the next hill. It was a safe way to live. His father called it a smart way, but Arlen thought differently. The people of Tibbet's Brook were too content to take someone else's word for what lay up the road or through the woods or past the river to the south . . . if there even *was* a river. Arlen preferred to see for himself.

How far could I get if I had all day? he always wondered. *How far, if I didn't have chores in the morning, if I didn't have to turn back and run halfway to dusk? Could I make it to safety before they came?* The thought thrilled and terrified him. What lay beyond the point of no return?

Maybe today I'll keep going.

But his resolve always faded as the sun rolled across the sky, and halfway to dusk, he inevitably felt his feet turning him around.

He slowed down when the house was in sight, despite the cries of his parents, despite the terror in their voices. This was the time of day he felt most alive. He watched the sun dip in the sky, eclipsed by the turning of the world beneath him. Shadows began to lengthen. He waited until the last minute, and then ran to his house as fast as he could, the exhilarating tingle of fear sweeping over him, making his heart pound and his hands shake. Air tasted better in those few seconds, his body alive with sensation. No sight was more beautiful than the reds and oranges of dusk, no sound more exciting than his parents' warnings. He tumbled over the threshold, careful not to disturb the wards, and turned to watch the corelings rise.

As the last warm rays faded from the horizon, and the heat leached from the ground into the air, the flame demons rose up from the Core to dance.

He was soon yanked inside and the heavy door shut, its bar thrown (as if it could stop a coreling!). Arlen's father would then check the wards on the sills and threshold again, making sure they had not been scuffed or scratched. He told Arlen that a triple-check was all that was needed, but he could never help checking a fourth time.

He was always scolded. Sometimes with his father's belt. But Arlen's parents knew deep down that no punishment could ever make him give up his wandering.

After punishment came supper, and then, while his

mother knit and his father carved wardposts, Arlen could sit by the window and watch the corelings dance. They were so graceful, even beautiful. Sometimes, he caught a glimpse of a wind demon, its shadowy form swooping on leathern wings, illuminated by the blazing eyes and mouths of its fiery cousins.

Less beautiful and thankfully less common were the rock demons, their hulking, sinewy forms encased in a carapace that could break the hardest spear tip. No dancers these, they stalked the yard slowly, flashing their rows of razor teeth as they searched for prey.

Arlen had never seen a water demon, but he had heard Jongleurs' stories. They could tear through the hull of a boat, dragging unfortunate fishermen under-water. Arlen shivered as he imagined the depths of the town lake swirling with dark, terrible forms. The idea terrified him, yet he longed to go out and try to glimpse one.

On some nights, the demons attacked the wards. They flung themselves at the doors and windows, only to be sent hurtling back by the flare of magic. Arlen's parents seldom flinched, having witnessed this all their lives.

"Why do they keep attacking when they can't get through?" Arlen asked his father once.

"They're looking for flaws in the net," his father replied, joining him by the window. "Every warding has them. Every one. Corelings aren't smart enough to study the wards and reason out the weak spots, but they can attack them and look for holes that way. You'll never see a coreling attack the same spot twice in a night." He tapped his temple. "They remember. And they know that time weakens even the strongest wards."

The night would light up over and over as the corelings tested the wards, magic flaring like tiny lightning flashes to momentarily illuminate the features of the yard as the demons tried to crush the well house, or reach the meat in the curing shed.

They attacked the barn as well, but the wards there were just as strong. Arlen could hear the livestock bleating in fear. The animals never got used to the demons. They knew, instinctively, what would happen if the corelings ever got through.

Arlen knew, too. When he was seven, he had watched helplessly as the demons tore apart one of their sheepdogs, spreading its guts all over the yard.

Corelings took great pleasure in killing.

It was said there had been a time when the demons were not so bold. A time when the greatest wards had not yet been forgotten; when the demons feared the power of mankind and stayed within the Core. But those days, if they ever truly existed, were long forgotten by the great-great-grandfathers of the oldest men alive. Now, those wards were nothing more than a Jongleur's tale.

As he watched the creatures that had stolen his world for another night, Arlen dreamed of bringing those wards back. He dreamed of traveling beyond Tibbet's Brook, and resolved that he would leave one day, even if it meant spending a night outside.

With the demons.

BRIANNE BEATEN

Introduction

This is far and away my favorite cut scene, my poor deleted darling. It takes place in Chapter 13 of *The Warded Man* ("There Must Be More"), and happens directly after the confrontation between Gared and Marick in the Cutter's Hollow marketplace. The purpose of the scene was to force Leesha to confront Brianne, who had been one of her best friends until the events of Leesha's first story arc destroyed their friendship. It was also meant to illustrate how confident and powerful Leesha had become during her Herb Gathering tutelage under Bruna.

Why It Was Cut

I take full responsibility for cutting this scene. No editor or agent or test reader suggested it. I needed to reduce the overall word count of the book, and as much as I loved this scene, it was more than 3,000 words and lifted out so cleanly that no one would ever miss it but me. That Leesha had grown too big for Cutter's Hollow was already apparent, and nothing else happened that affected the rest of the story at all.

I don't regret the decision. The final draft of the book is lean and mean, and every scene moves the story forward. This scene doesn't; it's just a tangent. Removing it also helped balance out the Leesha/Rojer airtime, which I had intended to be equal, but which was (and still is) skewed in Leesha's favor.

Still, I love this little side-story and am really happy I finally get to share it with people who might enjoy reading it.

"There's need for your skills," Mairy said.

"You feel unwell?" Leesha asked, concerned. She laid the back of her hand against Mairy's forehead, but Mairy shook her head, pulling away. "No, it's not for me," she said.

"One of the children?" Leesha asked, her eyes quickly scanning each for a sign of ill health. "Or Benn?"

Mairy shook her head again. "It's Brianne," she said. "She's been having stomach pains. She tries to hide it, but I see her wincing. Something is wrong. We hoped you might take the request for aid better from me."

"Why me?" Leesha asked. "Darsy is her Herb Gatherer."

"You've said yourself that Darsy guesses at her cures more oft than not," Mairy said. "And she lost Dug and Merrem's child last winter."

"I never said that was Darsy's fault," Leesha pointed out.

"You didn't have to," Mairy said. "Half the town is whispering it whenever she passes by. Brianne is just too proud to ask for your help."

"Even if she did," Leesha asked, "why should I give it?"

"Because she's sick and you're an Herb Gatherer," Mairy replied.

"She's spoken nothing but ill words on me for nearly seven years," Leesha said angrily. "And don't forget that she did her best to destroy my life." She turned away, but guilt ate at her. There were oaths Herb Gatherers took, to help all in need.

"She cried for you," Mairy said at her back. "We all did."

Leesha turned. "What do you mean?" she asked.

"That morning, when your mum came to town saying you ent come home before dark," Mairy said. "She had the whole town out looking for you or . . ." she looked away, "your body."

"We were sure you were dead," Mairy went on after

a moment, when Leesha did not reply. "Brianne said it was her fault, and fell into tears. We tried to tell her it wan't like that, but she was inconsolable." She touched Leesha's shoulder, "She knew she hurt you, Leesha."

"I never heard a word of contrition," Leesha said. "In fact, she's said worse about me since. Don't think I haven't heard."

"She meant to apologize," Mairy said. "Saira, too."

"But you were the only one that actually did," Leesha said.

"Hurting with words is easy," Mairy replied, echoing Leesha's earlier statement, "it's healing with them what's hard. Don't forget it was you what hurt her first."

Leesha felt as if she had been slapped in the face. What if Brianne was really sick and needed her help? Would she deny her? Deny her child? Had Bruna ever denied anyone?

"You're right," she told Mairy. "Of course I'll come help her."

"There's one other thing," Mairy said.

Leesha looked up.

"She's pregnant."

Mairy sent her little ones scurrying off home, and they headed for the small house the townsfolk had built when Brianne and Evin wed.

"How long has she known?" Leesha asked, walking

so fast that Mairy had to scurry to keep pace. Fear for Brianne's child gripped her.

"Her stomach told her a few weeks ago," Mairy said. "She might be as far as two months, now. She only told Evin this week."

"Were there any complications with her first pregnancy?" Leesha asked.

"Apart from being forced to marry Evin?" Mairy asked.

Leesha frowned at her.

"It's not funny, I know," Mairy said. "Callen's birth was easy. In fact, you might say it was the only easy thing about Callen."

"Because Evin didn't want him," Leesha said.

"That's putting it light," Mairy agreed. "Neither one was expecting the child. Brianne used to go to Bruna for pomm tea, but with you around . . . she said she couldn't bear the shame."

"She was one of the first to turn to Darsy," Leesha said.

"Only Darsy won't make the tea," Mairy said. "She says it's sinful, and told the Tender on the wives who'd been taking it. He gave a big sermon about our duty to procreate."

"I remember," Leesha said. Tender Michel had railed against pomm tea, but he had been careful not to say an ill word towards Bruna, lest the town learn how personally he took his duty.

"Well, that explains why Darsy is so busy as a

midwife," Leesha said. "Those that go to her are a lot more apt to need it."

"It's just as well," Mairy said. "There's few enough of us in Cutter's Hollow as is."

"Just as well, so long as she lets no more be born still," Leesha said.

"Brianne blames you, sometimes," Mairy blurted.

"Me?" Leesha asked. "What did I do?"

"Made her feel too shamed to get her pomm tea," Mairy said. "Made Evin have to marry her against his will. Made every day what's been bad since then."

"That isn't fair," Leesha said. "I was the one publicly humiliated because of her."

"Because of Gared," Mairy corrected.

"And Brianne got pregnant because of Evin, not me!" Leesha retorted.

Mairy nodded. "So maybe it's time to stop taking it out on each other," she said.

Leesha was quiet a long while. "I will if she will," she conceded at last.

"One of you has to be first," Mairy said.

Leesha stopped short. "Brianne doesn't know I'm coming," she said. When Mairy made no reply, she grinned. "Aren't you quite the little manipulator these days?" she accused.

"I get it from being a mum," Mairy confided with a giggle.

———————

Mairy took a deep breath and knocked on the door. There was noise from inside, but no one answered. Mairy knocked again.

"Who's that?" Evin cried.

"Mairy!" Mairy shouted.

There was some shouting inside. "Get it, yurself!" they heard Evin bark.

"Just come in!" Brianne called. "It ent barred!"

Mairy opened the door to reveal a squalid cabin. Two wolfhounds ran freely about the main room, and much of the furniture was gnawed upon. Evin sat with his muddy boots up on the supper table, whittling. The floor around him was covered in curls of wood. Brianne had her back to the door, chopping vegetables on the counter by the fire that served as her kitchen. Callen, six years old and tousle-haired, clung to her skirt with one hand. With the other, he rooted about one of his nostrils for some elusive prey.

"Sorry for the door, Mair," Brianne said without turning. "Creator forbid Evin fall behind at whittling useless sticks."

"Maybe a walk to the door once in a while would sweat off a few pounds," Evin muttered. "Whattaya want, anyway?" he asked, looking up and seeing Leesha enter.

"Well, well," he said, devouring Leesha with his eyes as he stood up suddenly, brushing the wood shavings from his clothes, "welcome to our humble home."

Brianne turned and saw her husband leering. She saw Leesha, and her face darkened.

"What is SHE doing here?!" Brianne demanded angrily, coming over with the chopping knife still in her hand.

"I thought she might be able to help with your pain," Mairy said.

"I didn't ask for any help," Brianne snarled. "It's nothing. I'm fine."

"I can see you're not," Leesha said. "Your coloring is off, your breathing's out of rhythm, and you grit your teeth when you walk."

"She said it's nothing," Evin said.

"Please," Mairy said. "Let her take a look. If not for you, think of the little one."

"The baby is fine," Evin said.

"Leave," Brianne said.

"Brianne . . ." Leesha began.

"Are you deaf?" Evin asked. "She said—"

"No," Brianne cut him off. "You. Leave."

"This is my house!" Evin sputtered, storming towards them, but Leesha put a hand in the pocket of her apron, and he noted the move, pulling up short.

"GET OUT!" Brianne screamed, throwing the knife at him. Evin ducked the missile and scowled, but he eyed Leesha's hand in her pocket, and headed for the door. Callen began to cry.

"And take those damn dogs with ya!" Brianne cried. "I'm tired of cleaning their shit off the floor!"

Evin clicked his tongue, and both animals followed him out of the cabin.

Brianne seemed to deflate as he left. She knelt in front of Callen, but grimaced in pain as she did. She lifted a corner of her apron to dry his tears.

"There, there, baby," she said. "It's all right. Run along and play with yur logs." She hugged him, and the boy ran over to the far corner of the room, where a pile of tiny sticks had been laid to form a crude miniature cabin.

Brianne stood, wincing again. Her face was ashen. "I suppose it makes ya feel good to see me like this," she told Leesha, "fat and miserable, while ya walk through town singing to the birds on yur shoulder and turning every man's head as ya go."

Leesha killed an angry retort before it reached her lips. "No one's suffering makes me feel good," she said. "Take a seat and let me have a look at you."

Brianne didn't argue, pain flashing across her face again as she sat. Leesha looked in her eyes and mouth, feeling her forehead for a fever and checking the pulse in her wrist.

"Let me know if anything I touch hurts," she said, and Brianne nodded. Leesha began to probe with sensitive fingers, watching Brianne's eyes the whole time. She already had her suspicions as to the cause of Brianne's pain.

"Aaah!" Brianne cried as Leesha pressed at her ribs.

"Take off your blouse," Leesha said.

"Is that really necessary?" Brianne asked.

"You were never shy about being naked back when we were friends," Leesha said.

"I was pretty then," Brianne shot back.

"Off with it," Leesha ordered. "Mairy, help me."

Brianne did not resist as the two pulled the blouse over her head. Mairy gasped at the yellowed bruises that covered Brianne's arms and back, and the black one, about as big as a palm-sized stone, on her ribs.

"It's just as I thought," Leesha said. "Two of your ribs are broken. You're lucky you didn't pop your lung."

"Can ya fix them?" Brianne asked.

Leesha shook her head. "There's not much to do for ribs but let them heal. I'll bind them so they heal straight and don't grind when you move, but you'll have to limit yourself for some time. Best altogether if you stay abed."

"Some time?" Brianne asked.

"Weeks," Leesha said, and she caught Brianne's look. "No arguing," she snapped. "We'll send someone to help you with Callen and around the house. You're lucky it's not worse."

"Creator!" Mairy said. "What happened, Bri?"

"I was standing on the woodpile, holding the paint can while Evin touched up the wards on the roof," Brianne said. "I slipped, and half the pile came down on me."

"Night!" Mairy exclaimed. "Why didn't you say something?"

"I thought I was fine," Brianne said.

"Look, I've got things here, Mair," Leesha said. "Why don't you get on home before the little ones get themselves into trouble?"

Mairy glanced at Brianne, who nodded her assent, and left.

"Demonshit," Leesha said when they were alone. "That son of a coreling beat you, and don't you think me stupid enough to believe any other tampweed tale you pull from your arse."

Brianne looked at her in shock. "Living with Bruna taught ya to curse," she said with a pained laugh. "Proper li'l Leesha I knew wun't have known what them words meant."

"Don't try to change the subject, either," Leesha said.

Brianne looked at her in fear. "What're ya gonna do?"

"Bind these ribs, to start," Leesha said. She took a roll of white cloth from her basket, and began wrapping it around Brianne's midsection, just below her breasts.

"Ahhh! Night, that stings!" Brianne gasped.

"Not half so much as the breaking itself, I'll wager," Leesha said. "Brianne, you have to tell someone. This can't go on."

"It was just the once," Brianne said.

Leesha snorted. "I don't believe that anymore than the woodpile tale," she said. "A man who'll hit a pregnant woman isn't new to the deed. Does Darsy know?"

Brianne shook her head. "No one knows. I never needed a Gatherer before."

"We have to put a stop to this before you need a Tender and a gravedigger," Leesha said.

"What would ya have me do?" Brianne demanded. "Tell my da? He and my brothers would kill Evin for this. They'd kill him for real, and be put out of the village at night for it. Callen would lose every man in his life over it, and where would I be?"

"Then tell Smitt," Leesha said. "Let the council handle it."

Brianne shook her head. "Da would still find out," she said, "and that would be that."

"So what?" Leesha demanded. "You let this go on until he does permanent harm to you or your unborn? Or Callen?"

"It won't happen again, Leesh," Brianne said, squeezing her hand, "he promised. Ya have to swear not to tell."

"Brianne . . ." Leesha began.

"Swear!" Brianne demanded, cutting her off. "Remember yur oath!"

Leesha's eyes narrowed, but she was trapped, and she knew it. Images flashed in her mind of Elona's belt, and how the pain had always seemed less than the shame of telling. "I swear," she said at last, grinding her teeth as she did.

She finished binding Brianne's ribs, and selected a handful of roots, holding them out. "Chew these for the pain," she said. "Only one a day, and no more, or the little one," she stroked Brianne's belly, "will make you regret it."

"Will the baby be all right?" Brianne asked, near tears.

"This time," Leesha said. "But if this happens again, who knows?"

"It won't, I swear," Brianne said.

"I don't think it's up to you," Leesha said.

Evin was in the yard when Leesha left. His eyes stroked her body, but he was wary, too. On impulse, Leesha went to him, putting an extra snap to the natural sway of her round hips.

"She's going to be fine," Leesha said. "That fall from the woodpile broke a couple of ribs, but they'll heal if she gets enough rest."

"The . . . woodpile," Evin began slowly, quickly gaining confidence as he caught on, "right. Awful spill. I told her to fetch a Gatherer, but ya know Brianne."

Leesha flashed him a bright smile. "I do at that," she said.

Evin returned the smile. "Yur looking good these days, Leesh," he breathed.

Leesha looked around. Seeing they were alone, she moved closer, standing on tiptoe so her lips practically touched his ear. "Come around the side of the house," she whispered. "I want to show you something."

Evin's grin split his face, and he grabbed her hand, practically dragging her along.

When they were alone, he was on her in an instant, kissing her hard and pawing her breasts. He didn't notice the needle in Leesha's hand until she stuck it in his neck.

"What the . . . !" Evin exclaimed, pulling away and slapping at the puncture. Already, he was starting to sway.

"The poison works fast," Leesha told him, straightening her blouse.

"Pois . . . ?" Evin started to ask, but then his feet went from under him, and he collapsed to the dirt, spasming erratically on his stomach.

"You feel that?" Leesha asked, kneeling beside him as his seizure began in earnest. "The horrid cramps and pain? Your limbs just twitching despite your commands for them to move?

"Don't worry, don't worry," she said, patting his back. "The poison will leave your muscles soon." She bent close, caressing his hair, and whispered, "It moves next into your gut."

Evin let out a low moan into the dirt.

"I promised Brianne I'd keep quiet about this," she said. "Herb Gatherers have an oath to hold secrets, and I'll not break that. But that doesn't mean I can't act on my own."

She gripped his hair tightly, forcing his head to turn towards her. "Look at me," she commanded. He tried weakly to pull away, but she held tight, pushing up his chin with her free hand to make him meet her eyes.

"You think hard," she said, "when you're screaming in the outhouse tomorrow. Think about how the next time I have to treat Brianne or one of the children because of you, you'll think of today as nothing. I'll make your bones scream, and your pathetic little dangle shrivel up like a raisin. I'll leave you hobbling on a cane before you see your thirtieth summer."

Evin looked at her, his eyes wide with terror. A lather of spit foamed out of his mouth, and a tear ran down his cheek.

She let go and stood. His head fell back to the dirt, flopping oddly.

"You think hard," she said again. Turning, she found herself face to face with Brianne.

She froze as Brianne looked down at her husband convulsing on the ground, and then back to Leesha. Their eyes met for what seemed like forever. Finally, Brianne nodded once.

Leesha nodded in return, and Brianne turned and went back into the cabin.

"Brianne is at least seven weeks pregnant," Leesha said. "She told Evin a week ago, and some time not long after, he beat her. The child is fine, but I treated two broken ribs and a number of bruises."

Bruna nodded as if Leesha had said nothing more than it looked like rain. "She begged you not to tell, I assume," she said.

"How did you know?" Leesha asked. Bruna raised an eyebrow at her, but didn't bother to reply.

"What did you do about it?" the crone asked.

"I stuck him with a needle dipped in slipsnake venom and told him I'd do worse the next time," Leesha said.

Bruna cackled and slapped her knee. "Couldn't have done better myself!" she howled. "Boy won't touch her again, and I wager he'll squirt his breeches the next time he sees you!"

"That was the idea," Leesha said, reddening.

"My children will be in good hands with you one day," Bruna said.

"No day soon, I hope," Leesha replied.

"Not for a while yet, at least," Bruna agreed, with a hint of sadness.

KRASIAN DICTIONARY

Abban: Wealthy *khaffit* merchant, crippled during his warrior training.

Alagai: Corelings, demons.

Alagai'sharak: Holy War against demonkind.

Amit: Crippled *dal'Sharum* with a peg leg who is Abban's principal rival in the Bazaar.

Anoch Sun: Lost city that was once the seat of power for Kaji. It was believed claimed by the sands. Its people and artifacts are called Sunian.

Asu: Son, or "son of." Used as a prefix in formal names.

Baha kad'Everam: Krasian hamlet renowned for its pottery, destroyed by demons in 306AR. The name translates as "Bowl of Everam." Its people are known as Bahavans.

Bazaar, Great: Merchant district of Krasia. It is run and frequented almost entirely by women and *khaffit*, because such business is considered beneath the warrior and clerical castes.

Camelpiss: Something or someone low and unworthy, vulgar.

Chabin: Father of Abban. *Khaffit*.

Chamber of Eternal Sorrow: Torture chamber in the underground tunnels beneath Sharik Hora used for heretics and traitors.

Chin: Outsider/infidel. Insulting connotation, implying that the person is a coward.

Couzi: A harsh, illegal Krasian liquor flavored with cinnamon. There is a brisk underground market, because a small, easily concealed flask will get several people drunk.

Dal'Sharum: Krasian warrior caste.

Dama: Krasian clerical caste. *Dama* are religious and secular leaders of Krasia. *Dama* wear white robes and carry no weapons. All are masters of *sharusahk* unarmed combat.

Damaji: Tribal leaders/high priests. Their council is the ruling body in Krasia.

Dama'ting: Krasian Priestesses and healers. Said to have magic powers, *dama'ting* are held in fear and awe by all outside their order.

Desert Spear, the: The Krasian term for their city, Fort Krasia.

Dravazi, Master: Famous pottery artisan from Baha kad'Everam. His fine pottery became priceless after his death.

Everam: The Creator.

Green lands: The lands north of the Krasian Desert.

Greenlander: One from the green lands.

Jamere: Abban's *nie'dama* nephew.

Kaji: The ancient Krasian leader who united the tribes

and then the known world in holy war against the demons. He is believed to have been the first Deliverer, who will come again.

Khaffit: Men who fail warrior training and are forced to take a craft. This is the lowest caste in Krasian society. *Khaffit* are forced to dress in the tan clothes of children and shave their beards as a mark of shame.

Nie'dama: Young clerical acolytes; *dama* in training. Literally "not *dama*."

Night veil: Veil worn by warriors to show unity and brotherhood in the night.

Par'chin: Literally "Brave outsider"; singular title for Arlen Bales to qualify that, though *chin*, he is no coward.

Pig-eater: Krasian insult meaning *khaffit*. Only *khaffit* eat pig, as it is considered unclean.

Sharik Hora: Temple made out of the bones of fallen warriors. Literally "Heroes' Bones."

Sharusahk: The Krasian art of unarmed combat.

Tribes: Krasia is divided into twelve tribes: Anjha, Bajin, Halvas, Jama, Kaji, Khanjin, Krevakh, Majah,

Mehnding, Nanji, Sharach, and Shunjin. One's tribe is considered part of one's name.

Undercity: Huge honeycomb of warded caverns beneath Fort Krasia where the women, children, and *khaffit* are locked at night to keep them safe from demons while the men fight.

WARD GRIMOIRE

Introduction

Wards are magical symbols whose origins are lost to history. Long thought to be the stuff of superstition, their power was rediscovered when, after an absence of thousands of years, the demon corelings returned to plague the surface of the world.

By themselves, wards have no power. Demons, however, are infused with core magic, and the fangs of a ward Draw that power, siphoning a portion away and repurposing the energy. The most common wards are defensive in nature, but a handful of wards that can achieve other effects are known, and, in theory, it is possible to create a ward for any desired effect. Recently, mankind has discovered offensive wards, which can actually harm demons, who are otherwise immune to hand weapons and can quickly recover from almost any injury.

Linked to one another in a closed circle, wards can distribute their effects and power evenly along the circumference.

Defensive Wards

Defensive wards draw magic from demons to form a barrier (forbiddance) through which the demons cannot pass. Wards are strongest when used against the specific demon type to which they are assigned, and are most commonly used in conjunction with other wards in circles of protection. When a circle activates, all demon flesh is forcibly banished from its line. Some examples:

Defensive Ward against: Bank Demons
First Appeared: *The Desert Spear*
Description: Called frog demons or "Froggies", these demons appear much like common fly frogs, but they are large enough to swallow humans whole. They lie in wait in shallow water, springing only when prey comes within range. One hop puts them up onto land, and they lash out with long, powerful tongues, catching

victims around the midsection or limbs and dragging them into the coreling's wide maw. Bank demons will then return to the water, drowning their struggling prey.

Defensive ward against: Clay Demons
First appeared: *The Great Bazaar*
Description: Clay demons are native to the hard clay flats on the outskirts of the Krasian Desert. Small, they are about the size of a medium-size dog, made from compact bunched muscle and thick, overlapping armor plates. They have short, hard talons that allow them to climb most any rock face, even hanging upside down. Their orange-brown armor can blend invisibly into an adobe wall or clay bed. The blunt head of a clay demon can smash through almost anything, shattering stone and denting fine steel.

Defensive Ward against: Field Demons
First Appeared: *The Daylight War*
Description: Sleek and low to the ground, with long, powerful limbs and retractable claws, field demons are

the fastest thing on four legs when they have open ground to accelerate. Tough scales on their limbs and back can turn most weapons, but if exposed, their underbelly is more vulnerable.

Defensive ward against: Flame Demons
First appeared: *The Warded Man*
Description: Flame demons have eyes, nostrils, and mouths that glow with a smoky orange light. They are the smallest demons, ranging from the size of a rabbit to that of a small boy. Like all demons, they have long, hooked claws and rows of razor-sharp teeth. Their armor consists of small, overlapping scales, sharp and hard. Flame demons can spit fire in brief bursts. Their firespit burns intensely on contact with air and can set almost any substance alight, even metal and stone.

Defensive Ward against: Lightning Demons
First Appeared: *The Daylight War*
Description: Nearly indistinguishable from their wind demon cousins, lightning demon spit is charged with

electricity that can paralyze a victim. They spit as they dive, snatching up their helpless prey to devour them alive.

Defensive ward against: Mimic Demons
First appeared: *The Desert Spear*
Description: Mimics are the elite bodyguards to mind demons (coreling princes) and are believed to be the most intelligent and powerful demons, short of the princes. Their natural form is unknown, but they are able to assume the form of any living thing, including other demon breeds, as well as clothing and equipment. These demons are somewhat lacking in creativity, and so are usually restricted to taking the forms of creatures they have themselves encountered (unless directed by a mind demon). One of their favorite tricks is to take the form of an injured human and feign distress to lower the defenses of their prey.

Defensive ward against: Mind Demons
First appeared: *The Desert Spear*

Description: Also known as coreling princes, mind demons are the generals of demonkind. They are physically weak, and have little in the way of the natural defenses of the other corelings, but they have vast mental and magical powers. They can read and control minds, communicate telepathically, and kill with their thoughts. By drawing wards in the air and powering them with their innate magic, they can create almost any effect. The other corelings, great and small, follow their every mental command without hesitation, and will give their lives to protect them. Sensitive to even reflected sunlight, mind demons will only rise on the three-night period of the new moon cycle in the hours when night is darkest.

Defensive ward against: Rock Demons
First appeared: *The Warded Man*
Description: The largest of the coreling breeds, rock demons can range in height from six to twenty feet tall. A hulking mass of sinew and sharp edges, their thick black carapaces are knobbed with bony protrusions, and their spiked tails can smash a horse's skull in a single blow. They stand hunched on two clawed feet, with long, gnarled arms ending in talons the size of butchering knives, and multiple rows of

bladelike teeth. No known physical force can harm a rock demon.

Defensive ward against: Sand Demons
First appeared: *The Warded Man*
Description: Cousins to rock demons, sand demons are smaller and more nimble, but still among the strongest and most armored of the coreling breeds. They have small, sharp scales that are a dirty yellow almost indistinguishable from gritty sand, and they run on all fours instead of two legs. Rows of segmented teeth jut out on their jaws like a snout, while their nostril slits rest far back, just below their large, lidless eyes. Thick bones from their brows curve upward and back, cutting through the scales as sharp horns. Their brows twitch continually as they displace the ever-blowing desert sand. Sand demons hunt in packs known as storms.

Defensive ward against: Snow Demons
First appeared: *Brayan's Gold*
Description: Similar to flame demons in build, snow

demons are native to frozen northern climates and high mountain elevations. Their scales are pure white, blending into the snow, and they spit a liquid so cold it instantly freezes anything it touches before evaporating. Steel struck with coldspit can become so brittle it shatters.

Defensive Ward: Succor
First Appeared: *The Warded Man*
Description: The succor ward is a general ward of protection taught to children. Not as powerful as wards keyed to individual breeds, succor wards create a general field of discomfort that is enough to drive most corelings away unless prey is in sight. The ward is used in the Thesan dice game Succor, as well as its Krasian variation, Sharak.

Defensive ward against: Swamp Demons
First appeared: *Messenger's Legacy*
Description: Swamp demons are native to swamps and marshy areas and are an amphibious form of wood

demon, at home both in the water and in the trees. Swamp demons are blotched in green and brown, blending in to their surroundings, and will often hide in trees, mud or shallow water to spring on prey. They spit a thick, sticky slime that rots any organic material it comes in contact with.

Defensive ward against: Water Demons
First appeared: *The Warded Man*
Description: Water demons vary in size and are seldom seen. They are long and scaly, with webbed hands and feet, tipped with sharp talons. Some breeds have tentacles ending in sharp bone. They can only breathe under water, though they can surface for a short time. Water demons can swim very quickly and delight in savaging fish, though they prefer warm-blooded mammals as their prey, especially those humans bold enough to dare to sail at night.

Defensive ward against: Wind Demons
First appeared: *The Warded Man*

Description: Wind demons stand about the height of a tall man at the shoulder, but with head fins that rise much higher, topping eight or nine feet. Their great long snouts are sharp-edged like beaks, but hide rows of teeth, thick as a man's finger. Their skin is a tough, flexible armor that can turn any spearpoint or arrowhead. That resilient substance stretches thin out from their sides and along the underside of their arm bones to form the tough membrane of their wings, which often span three times their height, jointed with wicked hooked talons that can cleanly sever a man's head when they dive. Clumsy and slow on land, wind demons have tremendous power in the sky and can dive, attack, and reverse direction before hitting the ground, taking their prey away with them.

Defensive ward against: Wood Demons
First appeared: *The Warded Man*
Description: Wood demons are native to forests. Next to rock demons, they are the largest and most powerful demons, averaging from five to ten feet tall when standing on their hind legs. They have short, powerful hindquarters and long, sinewy arms, perfect for climbing trees and leaping from branch to branch. Their claws are short, hard points, designed

for gripping through the bark of trees. Wood demons' armor is barklike in color and texture, and they have large black eyes. Wood demons cannot be harmed by normal fire, but will burn readily if brought in contact with hotter fires, such as magnesium or firespit. Wood demons will kill flame demons on sight, and often hunt in groups called copses.

Offensive (Combat) Wards

Combat wards siphon magic from a demon, weakening its armor at the point of contact, and redirect that magic as offensive force. This force can manifest in many different ways. Some examples:

Combat ward: Bludgeoning/impact
First appeared: *The Warded Man*
Description: This ward turns coreling magic into concussive force. The stronger the original blow, the more power generated. It can be placed onto any blunt weapon.

Combat ward: Cutting
First appeared: *The Warded Man*
Description: This ward, when etched along the length of a blade, can enhance its sharpness, allowing the weapon to cut cleanly through even coreling armor and flesh.

Combat ward: Heat
First Appeared: *The Warded Man*
Description: Heat wards Draw magic and convert it directly to heat. Objects painted with heat wards are consumed when the wards activate unless highly resistant to temperature extremes.

Combat ward: Piercing
First appeared: *The Warded Man*
Description: Piercing wards Draw from the point of

impact on a demon's body, weakening coreling armor even as they focus magic into a weapon's point for maximum penetrative power.

Combat ward: Pressure
First appeared: *The Warded Man*
Description: Pressure wards exert a crushing force that builds in heat and intensity the longer they remain in contact with a demon. The Warded Man has one on each palm, and has been known to squeeze a demon's head with them until it bursts.

Perception Wards

Perception wards create magical effects that can alter the senses of demons and sometimes humans.

Perception ward: Confusion
First Appeared: *The Warded Man*
Description: Confusion wards radiate a field of

disorientation that can cause demons to become dizzy and lose their sense of direction. Unless prey is in sight, drones will often forget what they are doing entirely, wandering away harmlessly.

Perception ward: Light
First Appeared: *The Desert Spear*
Description: Light wards Draw power from demons or ambient magic and convert it to pure white light. Depending on the power source, the light can be anything from a soft glow to a blinding glare.

Perception ward: Prophecy
First Appeared: *The Daylight War*
Description: Carved into the *alagai hora* of the *dama'ting*, prophecy wards read the currents of magic to make predictions about the future. Their magic pulls the demon bone dice out of their natural trajectories to answer questions spoken in prayer to Everam.

Perception ward: Unsight
First Appeared: *The Desert Spear*
Description: Rediscovered by Leesha Paper, wards of unsight can make objects and items invisible to demons, provided they keep relatively still. Hundreds, even thousands of wards of unsight are used to make cloaks and robes of unsight to protect humans in the naked night.

PETER V. BRETT is the bestselling author of The Demon Cycle, which includes *The Warded Man* (first published as *The Painted Man* in the UK by Del Rey Books), *The Desert Spear*, *The Daylight War* and *The Skull Throne*. The final book in the series, *The Core*, is expected in 2017. In addition to the quintet, he has published three novellas, *The Great Bazaar*, *Brayan's Gold*, and *Messenger's Legacy*, as well as *Red Sonja: Unchained* and *Red Sonja: Blue* for Dynamite Comics.

Raised on a steady diet of fantasy novels, comic books, and *Dungeons & Dragons*, Brett has been writing fantasy stories for as long as he can remember. He received a bachelor of arts degree in English literature and art history from the University at Buffalo in 1995, then worked for a decade in pharmaceutical publishing before returning to his bliss. He lives in Manhattan.

Visit Peter online at www.petervbrett.com or follow him on Twitter @PVBrett